AN IMPROMPTU PROPOSAL

Carla Cassidy

Silhouette
R O M A N C E™
Published by Silhouette Books
America's Publisher of Contemporary Romance

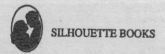

SILHOUETTE BOOKS

ISBN 0-373-19152-9

AN IMPROMPTU PROPOSAL

"Please, Mr. Graves.
Please find Sam for me."

"I'll see what I can do," he answered gruffly, oddly touched by her.

As he watched her walk away again he noticed the shapely length of her legs beneath her dress. Definitely an attractive woman. He wondered if Sam Baker had chosen to walk away from her....

Colleen. She was a bundle of contradictions. And those eyes, so blue and glittering with such deep emotion. They were the kind of eyes that could haunt a man. From the moment he'd gazed into them, he'd known he would take the case....

Dear Reader,

Take one married mom, add a surprise night of passion with her almost ex-husband, and what do you get? *Welcome Home, Daddy!* In Kristin Morgan's wonderful Romance, Rachel and Ross Murdock are now blessed with a baby on the way—and a second chance at marriage. That means Ross has only nine months to show his wife he's a FABULOUS FATHER!

Now take an any-minute-mom-to-be whose baby decides to make an appearance while she's snowbound at her handsome boss's cabin. What do you get? *An Unexpected Delivery* by Laurie Paige—a BUNDLES OF JOY book that will bring a big smile.

When one of THE BAKER BROOD hires a sexy detective to find her missing brother, she never expects to find herself walking down the aisle in Carla Cassidy's *An Impromptu Proposal.*

What's a single daddy to do when he falls for a woman with no memory? What if she's another man's wife—or another child's mother? Find out in Carol Grace's *The Rancher and the Lost Bride.*

Lynn Bulock's *And Mommy Makes Three* tells the tale of a little boy who wants a mom—and finds one in the "Story Lady" at the local library. Problem is, Dad isn't looking for a new Mrs.!

In Elizabeth Krueger's *Family Mine*, a very eligible bachelor returns to town, prepared to make an honest woman out of a single mother—but she has other ideas for him....

Finally, take six irresistible, emotional love stories by six terrific authors—and what do you get? Silhouette Romance—every month!

Enjoy every last one,

Melissa Senate
Senior Editor

Please address questions and book requests to:
Silhouette Reader Service
U.S.: 3010 Walden Ave., P.O. Box 1325, Buffalo, NY 14269
Canadian: P.O. Box 609, Fort Erie, Ont. L2A 5X3

Books by Carla Cassidy

Silhouette Romance

Patchwork Family #818
Whatever Alex Wants... #856
Fire and Spice #884
Homespun Hearts #905
Golden Girl #924
Something New #942
Pixie Dust #958
The Littlest Matchmaker #978
The Marriage Scheme #996
Anything for Danny #1048
Deputy Daddy #1141
Mom in the Making #1147
An Impromptu Proposal #1152

Silhouette Desire

A Fleeting Moment #784
Under the Boardwalk #882

*The Baker Brood

Silhouette Shadows

Swamp Secrets #4
Heart of the Beast #11
Silent Screams #25
Mystery Child #61

Silhouette Intimate Moments

One of the Good Guys #531
Try To Remember #560
Fugitive Father #604

Silhouette Books

*Silhouette Shadows
  Short Stories* 1993
"Devil and the Deep Blue Sea"

The Loop

Getting it Right: Jessica

CARLA CASSIDY

is the author of ten young-adult novels, as well as many contemporary romances. She's been a cheerleader for the Kansas City Chiefs football team and has traveled the East Coast as a singer and dancer in a band, but the greatest pleasure she's had is in creating romance and happiness for readers.

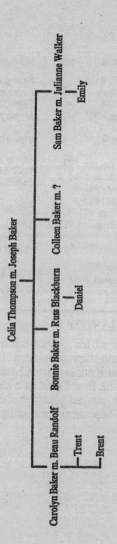

The Baker Brood

Celia Thompson m. Joseph Baker

Carolyn Baker m. Beau Randolf
— Trent
— Brent

Bonnie Baker m. Russ Blackburn
Daniel

Colleen Baker m. ?

Sam Baker m. Julianne Walker
Emily

Chapter One

Gideon Graves had suffered hangovers in the past, but even before opening his eyes, he knew this one was going to be the mother of all hangovers. He groaned softly, a vague memory of clams on half shells and shots of tequila filtering through his mind. Somebody had gotten married, but at the moment he couldn't remember who it had been. He only remembered toasting the bride, the groom, the future, the past . . . whatever.

Without opening his eyes, he knew it was still early. He could hear the sound of fishing boats taking off, their wakes causing his little houseboat to rock gently to and fro like an unborn baby in a womb.

He groaned and rolled over, his hand automatically seeking a pack of cigarettes from the bedside stand. Instead his fingers closed around a package of candy, reminding him he'd quit the smoking habit a week before.

"Damn," he grumbled and pulled out a twist of the red licorice. Popping the end of it into his mouth, he chewed thoughtfully, wondering how long it would be before the hangover headache disappeared. And how long would it be before the next job appeared? He'd finished his last assignment two weeks ago, and so far nothing new had cropped up. However, he wasn't worried. He was good at what he did, and sooner or later somebody would need his particular skills. Besides, his head hurt too much to think too long or hard on any subject.

What he needed was another couple of hours of sleep. He hadn't stumbled to bed until nearly four, and it couldn't be much later than six now.

Finishing the licorice, he snuggled deeper beneath the blanket and fell easily into a deep, dreamless sleep. It felt as if he'd only been asleep a moment when he heard a light rapping on the door. "Go away," he growled hoarsely, then moaned and gripped the sides of his head to keep it from rolling off his shoulders.

The knock came again, this time louder, more persistent.

"Damn." Gideon cracked open his eyes, squinting at the early morning sunshine that streamed in the round porthole window. Gazing at his alarm, he saw it was just after eight o'clock. Who in the hell would be at his door at this hour?

Groaning again, he stumbled out of bed and yanked on a pair of sweatpants. If the tenacious knocker was Fast Eddy he'd wring the kid's scrawny little neck. "What?" he barked as he threw open his door.

"Mr. Graves? Gideon Graves?"

His early morning caller definitely wasn't the teenage boy. Although the sun was at her back, making it impossible to see her features, her voice was low and musical, infinitely appealing. Even more appealing was the fact that the sun shone through her lightweight, gauzy dress, displaying the outline of distinctly feminine, shapely legs. "Yeah, what do you want?"

There was a momentary pause. "Are you Gideon Graves? The private investigator?"

"None other. Who are you?" There was something about the slightly arrogant edge to her voice that rankled him, but not as much as her shapely legs intrigued him.

"My name is Colleen Jensen. I'm sorry to bother you so early, but I was on my way to work and decided to stop by. I have a private matter I'd like to discuss with you."

"Do I owe you money?"

"No."

Ignoring the dull thud of his headache, Gideon opened the door to allow her entrance. "Excuse the mess," he said, sweeping beer bottles, pizza boxes and fast food cartons off the table and onto the floor. "I'd

tell you my cleaning lady quit, but the truth is I never
had one.''

He turned around, vaguely irritated to see she
hadn't followed, but instead still stood just outside the
door, as if preparing herself to enter a den of iniquity.
''You coming or going, lady?'' he asked, his exasperation growing. Who needed this at eight in the morning, especially on top of a monster hangover?

The woman stepped inside, carefully picking her
way around discarded clothing and trash. She made
her way to the table, then sat down, the corners of her
lips curled disdainfully downward.

Gideon sat across from her, saying nothing, taking
her full and total measure in a minute. Money. She
smelled of it. As far as Gideon was concerned there
were two types of people. The ones who had money
and the ones who wanted everyone to think they had
money.

People with money wore their mink on the inside.
People without money flashed it outwardly, not understanding the hundreds of little ways they gave
themselves away.

Colleen Jensen was definitely the first type. She
wore expensive shoes and carried an expensive purse,
two areas where pretenders normally skimped. Her
short dark hair had a quality cut, although he wasn't
sure if the curls were natural or permed. Her dress was
designer issue, a classical style that would stay in
fashion for years.

Even if she had been naked, he would have guessed she came from a background of wealth. It was in the haughty lift of her dark eyebrows, the way she sat patiently, obviously waiting for him to speak first. Oh, yeah, he smelled money, all right, and it intensified his headache. To Gideon Graves, money smelled like betrayal.

She shifted uncomfortably in the folding chair, her blue eyes gazing at him somewhat dubiously. "Are you really as good as they say?"

"It depends on who they are and which of my particular talents they were discussing." He smiled, knowing the gesture didn't reach his eyes. "I've been told I have many talents."

A pale pink blush stained her cheeks. "And I've been told that you're one of the best at finding people who are missing."

He sat up straighter in his chair, as always a burst of adrenaline sprinting through him at the possibility of a case. "Who's missing?"

"His name is Sam Baker."

"And what is this Sam Baker to you?" Gideon asked, looking around for a notepad, a blank piece of paper, anything he could write on. He finally settled on a take-out sack from a nearby pizza place. Smoothing out the wrinkles, he wrote down the name Sam Baker, then looked at her again, aware she hadn't answered his last question. "Your relationship to Sam Baker?" he repeated.

The pink of her cheeks intensified. "Look, I love him and that's all you need to know."

"And what makes you think he's seriously missing rather than simply missing from your life? Did you have a lovers' spat? Anything like that?"

He could tell the question angered her. The blue of her eyes deepened, and her lips compressed together tightly. "No spats, no fights. If it was at all possible, Sam would have been in touch with me, and I haven't heard from him in three months. I want to find him. I need to find him."

Three months. Renewed adrenaline pumped. The longer a person was missing, the more difficult the case. And Gideon thrived on challenge. Again he looked at the woman across from him, assessing, probing. Had this Sam Baker been her ticket to a nicer life-style? Was that why she wanted him found?

"Why do you want me to find him?" He asked the question that was in his head.

She looked at him in surprise. "I already told you. Because I love him."

He didn't doubt it. The love shone from her eyes, and for a split second, Gideon envied Sam Baker, wherever he was. "When was the last time anyone saw Sam?"

She withdrew a manila folder from her oversize purse. "Everything is in here. All the information you should need." She held on to the folder for another moment. "How much is your fee?"

He told her what he charged, noting she didn't flinch. "Before I agree to take the case, I need to look over all the information you've provided."

She nodded and stood. "If you decide to take the case, I'd, uh, appreciate discretion." Another blush stained her cheeks as she averted her gaze. "Sam is married." She looked at him. "Can I call you this evening?"

He got up, as well, and wrote down his number on a piece of the bag. He ripped it off and handed it to her. "If I'm not here leave your number and I'll get back to you."

He walked her to the door and was suddenly aware of her perfume. It filled the air with a sweet floral scent, a welcome relief from the stale air inside the houseboat.

When they got to the door, she turned to him, her eyes shimmering with unexpected emotion. "Please, Mr. Graves. Please find Sam for me."

"I'll see what I can do," he answered gruffly, oddly touched by the depth of the emotion shining from her eyes.

As he watched her walk down the dock toward the parking area in the distance, again he noticed the shapely length of her legs beneath the cotton material of her dress. Definitely an attractive young woman. He wondered if Sam Baker had chosen to walk away from her.

He turned and went inside, his thoughts remaining on Colleen Jensen. She'd been a bundle of contradictions, giving him the illusion of a wealthy background, yet concerned enough to ask about his fee. And those eyes, so blue and glittering with such deep emotion. They were the kind of eyes that could haunt a man. The moment he'd gazed into them, he'd known he would take the case.

Consciously steering away from the manila envelope on the table, he instead opted to make coffee. Perhaps a cup of strong brew would dilute the headache still pounding at his temples.

The coffee had just finished perking when another knock sounded on his door. Now what? He stifled a groan as he opened the door and saw the gangly teenager grinning widely at him. Fast Eddy.

"Hi, Gideon, I saw the dame leaving. Is she a new customer?" Eddy followed Gideon in, his face radiating the eager friendliness of a puppy dog.

"Client, Eddy, not customer," Gideon replied as he poured himself a cup of the fresh brew.

"So, what kind of work does she want you to do? Is she in trouble? Is she wanted by the mob? Is somebody blackmailing her?" Eddy pulled a kitchen chair out and straddled it, his shoulders pumped in adolescent machismo.

"Eddy, you've been reading too many Mike Hammer novels. She is not a dame, and she wants me to find someone for her." Gideon joined him at the table, vaguely wondering how he had become surrogate father and friend to the red-haired teenager.

"So, are you gonna take her case?" He leaned forward, his features animated in the way only youth and innocence could produce. "Maybe I could help. You know, be your backup...your partner."

Gideon frowned. "Isn't it September? Shouldn't you be in school?"

"Nah. I graduated last May." He paused a moment, watching as Gideon took a sip of his coffee, then continued, "I've been kind of thinking it would be great to work for you. You know, sort of a P.I. in training. You wouldn't have to pay me much, and I could really be a big help."

It was the puppy-dog eagerness on Eddy's face that made Gideon swallow his initial, vehement negative reply. The last thing Gideon needed was an overzealous teenager shadowing his every move, fantasizing himself the new detective extraordinaire. He took another drink of his coffee. And yet, he knew enough about Fast Eddy's dismal home life to realize the kid had little else going for him.

He drained his coffee, then went into the bathroom where he washed up, then pulled on a pair of soft, worn jeans and grabbed a clean shirt from the closet. He walked into the living room, aware of Eddy's gaze on him as he fastened the shirt buttons. One part hero worship, one part studied nonchalance, Eddy observed his every move as if memorizing it to mimic later.

He wanted to yell at the kid, tell him to find somebody else to bother, a real hero to emulate, not some burned-out ex-cop whose buddies had turned their backs on him.

It irritated Gideon that he just couldn't yell at the kid, couldn't tell him to go away, because Gideon could feel the loneliness that radiated inside the kid. It mirrored the loneliness he tried to ignore deep within himself.

"Look, Eddy," he said as he pulled on socks and stepped into his shoes. "My caseload is kind of light right now, and I really don't need that kind of help." Gideon straightened up, looking around in disgust. "What I definitely need is a maid," he muttered, more to himself than to his youthful companion.

"I can do that," Eddy exclaimed. Before Gideon could protest, Eddy jumped out of his chair and started picking up trash from the floor. "It's sort of like starting at a lower-level entry kind of job." Eddy gathered an armful of dirty dishes and placed them in the sink. "I'll start here, and when you think I'm ready and your caseload gets heavier, I'll be here to help you with the detective work."

Gideon had the horrifying sensation of his life suddenly out of control. He had a mental vision of a pair of blue eyes demanding he get right to work and a more horrifying mental picture of a red-haired scrawny teenager taking over his home. He grabbed the manila folder off the top of the table. "I've got something to check out. I'll be back later."

"No problem," Eddy said agreeably. He walked with Gideon to the door. "Don't worry about a thing. I'll hold down the fort while you're gone."

"Just lock up when you leave," Gideon said, fighting another wave of nauseating head pounding.

"Oh, don't worry about that. I'll just hang around until you get back." Eddy grinned widely. "See ya later, partner."

Swallowing a grunt of resignation, Gideon left the little houseboat that had been his home for the past seven years. His thoughts once again turned toward Colleen Jensen. Before he agreed to take on the case of the missing Sam Baker, he intended to do a little checking up on the attractive Ms. Jensen. There was one thing he had learned in his life... trust nobody. And the last person in the world he would ever trust was a gorgeous damsel in distress with haunting blue eyes.

He grinned, then sobered just as quickly. He had to do something about Eddy. If he didn't take control of that particular situation quickly, he had a feeling Fast Eddy would be moved in, lock, stock and barrel, before Gideon could blink an eye.

As he thought of sharing his private space with the eager, talkative teen, his headache throbbed full force. It looked like it was going to be one of those days.

"Amy, I'm so proud of you." Colleen praised the young woman who sat in front her, a baby in one arm and a toddler hanging on to her knees. "Getting your high-school equivalency is the best gift you can give yourself."

The young woman smiled shyly. "My next goal is to get a good job. My mom has agreed to watch the kids for me so I can work and get a better place to live. I want to get out of that tiny apartment, maybe find something with a yard for the kids."

"It sounds like you're making good choices." Colleen smiled, noting that both children were clean and looked well-fed. She hoped this woman, at seventeen, little more than a child herself, and her children would be one of the success stories.

"Well, I guess that does it for now." Colleen closed the file folder and stood up. "I'll be in touch over the next couple of weeks. Don't hesitate to call if you or the children need anything."

She escorted the woman out of the small office, then went back to her desk and flopped down in exhaustion. Looking at her watch, she realized it was nearly two. She'd worked through lunch...as usual.

She looked up as a knock sounded, and then her door opened. Smiling at the older woman who peeked in, Colleen gestured to the chair in front of her desk. "Margie, come in and take a load off."

Margie Mayfield, Colleen's co-worker and friend, walked in and perched one slender hip on the edge of Colleen's desk. "I saw Amy leaving. She doing all right?"

Colleen smiled. "She's doing terrific. She got her GED yesterday."

"Good for her." Margie shook her head, her shoulder-length strawberry-colored hair dancing with the motion. "Chalk one up for the good guys. Hard to believe a year ago we thought we were going to have to take her kids away from her."

Colleen grinned. "But isn't it nice to have a success story for a change?" As social workers dealing with child protection and rights, Colleen and Margie saw far too few success stories.

"My real question is, did you hire that private eye guy I told you about?"

Colleen's smile instantly passed as she thought of her early morning visit to Gideon Graves. "I stopped by and spoke to him this morning." She'd consciously kept thoughts of him at bay since arriving at the office, but now her mind filled with the memory of the big man, with his wild hair and scandalously tight cotton sweatpants. "I have to confess, I wasn't real impressed. He lives on a houseboat, and it was a complete mess."

Margie shrugged. "Why do you care if he lives in a mess? You don't want him to live with you, you just want him to find Sam."

Yes, desperately, Colleen wanted him to find Sam. It had been months since she'd seen him, talked to him, known that he was all right. The circumstances surrounding Sam's disappearance were horrifying, and a hollow ache pained Colleen's heart.

"So what did you tell this private eye?"

"Not much," Colleen admitted. "I just told him Sam had disappeared. He thinks Sam's my lover."

Margie scowled. "You should have told him the truth."

Colleen felt the heat that rose to her face. "I've hired three other detectives, and when they found out I'm Sam's sister and part of the Baker dynasty, their prices tripled, and I still got no results. They took advantage of me because I'm a Baker, and I'm not going to let that happen again."

"Don't you think Gideon Graves will discover the truth? That you aren't Sam's lover, and that Sam is a fugitive from justice because he's suspected of the murder of your father?"

"If he's any good, he'll eventually find all that out. But I'm not convinced the man I spoke to this morning could find his way out of a paper sack," Colleen said dryly.

"Everyone I've spoken to told me he's the best of the bunch."

Colleen smiled. "But being the best of the bunch isn't saying much if the rest of the bunch is all rotten."

Margie laughed and stood up. "I just hope you know what you're doing."

"Of course I do," Colleen answered firmly. It wasn't until Margie left the office that Colleen admitted to herself she had absolutely no idea what she was doing.

All she did know was that she had to do something to try to find Sam. Her brother's absence in her family's life was a daily heartache.

She got up from her desk. Over the past few months, her life had been a roller-coaster ride, with dizzying highs and horrifying lows. The horror had started with the murder of her father. He'd been found dead in his office at the Baker Enterprises building, and an eyewitness had reported seeing Sam running from the scene of the crime. In one fell swoop, Colleen had lost both her father and her brother. Although there was no doubt in her mind that Sam hadn't committed the crime, she didn't understand why he didn't come back and defend himself against the accusations and speculation.

She stared out her office window, the Bay Shore and Long Island marina barely visible in the distance. If she was just a little bit closer, she would be able to see Gideon Grave's rickety houseboat. She frowned as she remembered the vessel. By the looks of it, she was surprised it was seaworthy. If Gideon Graves was one of the best, he certainly didn't live like a success.

Still, Margie was right. Colleen didn't care if Gideon Graves lived in a hole in the ground, if he could only help her.

Would Gideon Graves finally get her some answers about her brother? She certainly didn't feel particularly optimistic about the bloodshot-eyed, wild-haired detective. He'd looked like he'd been on a month-long drunk and resented getting sober.

Turning away from the window, she reached up and touched the necklace that hung around her neck. Her fingers closed around the charm in the shape of the mythical phoenix. Her father had given one to each of his children right before his death. Clasping it in her fingers should have sent sorrow and grief for her father sweeping through her, but it was hard to grieve for a man who'd been little more than a distant stranger to his youngest child.

It had been Sam who had kissed her childhood boo-boos and given her heartfelt advice. It had been her big brother who had soothed her fears and dried her tears. She'd been closer to him than to either of her sisters. His absence from her life had left a gnawing black hole in the center of her heart, a hole she feared would never be filled again.

Whatever it took. She would do whatever it took to find Sam. Even if it meant dealing with a man like Gideon Graves. Shivering slightly, she moved away from the window, her thoughts once again filled with visions of the private investigator.

She didn't exactly have a wonderful opinion about private investigators. Her brief experiences with the three she had previously hired had been horrendous. Still, Gideon Graves hadn't been what she'd expected. The other three she'd subsequently fired had all been older, softer. Gideon was definitely different.

He'd filled the small confines of the houseboat with his presence, a presence that radiated undeniable masculinity and an underlying hint of danger. But was he any good? Would he be able to get her some answers about Sam or would he just make empty promises as the others had and suck as much money as possible out of her? Only time would tell.

She sank down on her chair behind her desk, her gaze once again drifting out the window. She was desperate enough, hurting enough that at this point she'd throw her lot in with the very devil himself if he could find Sam. What she didn't understand was why, when she thought of working with Gideon Graves, she had the distinct feeling she'd done just that.

Chapter Two

Gideon slid farther down in the seat behind the steering wheel, staring at the ornate iron gates that led to the elusive Sam Baker's house.

Sam Baker was obviously a wealthy man...wealthy enough to maintain a fairly fancy house. It was an older, two-story home that whispered of wealth rather than shouted it. The grounds behind the gate were well-kept, furthering the aura of a carte-blanche existence.

Even if Colleen hadn't told him, it had been easy to discern that Sam was married. The mailbox had the names Mr. and Mrs. Sam Baker on it. A tricycle in the driveway was mute evidence of a child or children. So, Sam Baker had a wife and child, and apparently a mistress who missed him desperately.

Gideon frowned as his mind filled with the memory of Colleen Jensen. Why would a woman with her good looks and intelligence settle for half a life with a married man? Why would she want the back streets, stolen moments and borrowed happiness of being a mistress? Money. The obvious answer came unbidden to his mind.

Shifting positions to ease cramping legs, he reached into the glove box and grabbed a piece of licorice. Once again he settled back against the seat. He'd never understood what motivated women to become involved with married men. Or single men to become involved with married women. Personally, Gideon considered himself far too selfish for such a relationship. He would never settle for sharing. Besides, he believed in fidelity. He might have made a lot of mistakes in his failed marriage, but cheating wasn't one of them.

He finished the licorice stick and reached for another. This was the part of his job he hated, the sitting, waiting, watching. Unfortunately, he had yet to figure out a better, more efficient way to get the facts he needed. And right now what he needed to figure out was exactly what Colleen Jensen wanted.

One thing Gideon had learned early in this life was that people were rarely honest, and there were always ulterior motives hidden beneath their surfaces. Colleen had maintained that she wanted Sam found because she loved him, but Gideon had seen the whisper of secrets in the depths of her eyes, secrets that had intrigued him.

He straightened in the seat as he saw a police car cruising toward him. The car moved slowly, then parked at the curb in front of the Baker residence, directly across from where Gideon was parked.

Terrific. Gideon groaned, wondering if one of the neighbors had called him in as a suspicious car and occupant. As the officer in the passenger side of the car got out and approached him, he groaned again, immediately recognizing the arrogant walk and sharp features of the uniformed man.

"Well, well, well, if it isn't Long Island's fallen angel."

Gideon smiled tightly. "Good morning, Ed. What brings Suffolk County's finest to this neck of the woods?"

The officer shrugged. "This and that." He eyed Gideon speculatively. "What about you?"

Gideon mimicked him. "This and that." Officer Ed Sanders had been one of the initial fellow officers to turn his back on him when Gideon had been on the force and the first of the ugly rumors had surfaced. Although three years had passed since that time, Gideon rarely forgave, and he never forgot.

"You working on the Sam Baker case?" Although the question was asked nonchalantly, Gideon knew Ed well enough to know he never did anything casually.

"Maybe." Gideon was an old hand at poker playing and knew his features didn't indicate his surprise that the police were interested in the elusive Sam Baker. "You know where he is?"

Ed snorted. "I wish. If we knew, we wouldn't be running surveillance here every time things get slow." He leaned against the car door, a pleasant smile on his face. "So, who's your client?"

Gideon laughed. "Now, Ed, you know I can't tell you that."

Ed's ferret features twisted in mock surprise. "Ethics? Why, Gideon, I didn't know you had any."

Gideon laughed again, ignoring the burn of resentment in his chest. "Go to hell, Ed." He started the car and put it into gear. He inched forward, forcing the officer to step back from the door. "See you around, Ed," he called out the window as he pulled away from the curb.

"Damn," he exclaimed as he hit his palm against the steering wheel. It was obvious Ms. Sexy Legs had left out some important facts in the information she'd provided him.

He cursed himself as well as her. Generally, he did preliminary investigations at the library, the courthouse, wherever he thought he could get background information on the subject. However, when he'd left the house, his headache had still raged, and he'd decided to go to the address provided by Colleen and simply get his own impressions of the subject's home.

Obviously Sam Baker was more than just a missing person. Typically, missing persons didn't garner police surveillance on their homes. So, what exactly had Legs forgotten to tell him?

Nearly two hours later, he had many of the pieces filled in. Gideon turned off the microfilm machine and reared back in his chair, trying to decide what to do.

The library was relatively empty. Other than himself and the dour-looking librarian, an old gentleman thumbing through magazines was the only person present.

The silence was conducive to thought, and Gideon's brain raced with the information he'd just gleaned. Sam Baker was not just missing, he was a fugitive from the law. The newspaper articles had named him the main suspect in the death of his father, Joseph Baker. Joseph Baker hadn't been just an ordinary, hardworking citizen. He'd been the head of a multimillion-dollar industry. Now the police presence outside Sam Baker's home made more sense.

What didn't make sense was why Colleen Jensen had neglected to add this little tidbit of information to her notes. A rather glaring omission, Gideon thought wryly.

Perhaps it was time to do a little digging into Colleen Jensen. For all he knew, that wasn't her real name. She could be anyone, even a police officer on the case, stymied by a lack of leads and willing to do anything to break the case...even make a pact with the fallen angel of Long Island.

The fallen angel of Long Island. Gideon's stomach clenched as he remembered Ed's words. He'd known that was how most of the members of the police department referred to him behind his back. The fallen angel. The tarnished badge. The one who went bad.

His whole career as a police officer had blown up in his face, leaving him bitter, angry and a much smarter man. The beginning of the end had been when he'd met Anne. Amazing how blind love could be, how it twisted beliefs, skewed vision and caused bad choices.

The biggest mistake of his life had been falling in love. It was a mistake he never intended to repeat. Shoving aside the unpleasant memories, he stood up, deciding it was time to get back to work.

Colleen uttered a grateful sigh as she pulled into the driveway of the duplex she owned. She smiled as she saw Mrs. Blankenship, the elderly widow who rented the other half of the building, watering the remains of the late summer flowers that bordered the front of the structure. God bless Elda Blankenship. Her green thumb kept the front of the building resplendent with color.

Getting out of her car, she greeted the older woman with a smile and a wave. "Evening, Elda."

"You worked late again, Colleen. You're too young and pretty to spend so many hours at work." Elda leaned down and turned off the spigot, then efficiently wrapped the garden hose into a neat little circle.

"I love my job," Colleen answered, knowing what Elda's next statement would be. This was a conversation they had often. From anyone else it would have irritated Colleen, but she knew Elda's sole motivation was genuine affection.

"A job won't keep you warm on cold wintry nights," Elda observed, just as Colleen had anticipated she would.

She smiled. "No, but an electric blanket will, and it won't give me any grief."

Elda chuckled and shook her head. "You're a stubborn one, Colleen Jensen."

"I suppose I am," Colleen replied grudgingly. She reached into the car to gather the files she'd brought home, then slammed the car door.

"Before you go inside, I've got something for you." Elda disappeared into her half of the duplex and returned a moment later with a paper bag that smelled of cinnamon and yeasty dough. "I baked this morning, and I know how much you love my cinnamon knots."

Colleen gave the woman a quick hug, as always thanking her stars that she'd found such a wonderful tenant. "Thank you, you're much too good to me," she exclaimed as she released Elda.

Elda smiled. "Somebody needs to be good to you, you certainly aren't good to yourself." She looked pointedly at the files Colleen held in her arms. "You look tired. You'd be better off forgetting that work and going straight to bed."

"I just might do that," Colleen agreed, then telling her neighbor goodbye, she unlocked her front door.

When she stepped inside, the hues of twilight seeping in through the windows painted the living room in warm, golden tones. It was good to be home. She immediately turned on the lamp next to the sofa, knowing that at this time of the year, twilight didn't last long and darkness fell quickly.

Throwing the files and the paper bag from Elda on the polished surface of the coffee table, she sank down on the sofa and kicked off her shoes. Perhaps Elda had a good idea. Maybe Colleen should just forget working tonight and go to bed. She was exhausted.

She reached for the bag, the scent of cinnamon once again wafting. Her stomach rumbled in hunger, reminding her she'd skipped lunch. She reached inside the bag, pulled out one of the baked sweets and bit into it, thinking once again of the frantic work schedule she'd been keeping.

What Elda didn't understand, couldn't understand about Colleen's work was that it had been her escape, her sanity. At least while dealing with clients, reading case files and making important decisions, she couldn't think about Sam.

Thinking of him, she reached for her purse. She'd hoped to come home to a message on her answering machine from Gideon Graves, telling her he was taking the case. But the red light on her machine wasn't blinking to announce any calls. Digging through the contents of her purse, she retrieved the slip of paper the private detective had given her with his phone number written on it.

Instead of dialing his number right away, she leaned back into the couch cushions, staring thoughtfully at his bold, strong writing. In the brief time she'd spent with Gideon Graves, he'd unsettled her as she hadn't been unsettled in a very long time.

He'd been so blatantly masculine, with just enough rough edges to make him intriguing. A dangerous combination and a definite strike against pursuing him to take the case. She'd tried that particular combination before, with heartbreaking results.

Still, after being burned by the three other private detectives, she'd done a lot of checking on Gideon Graves before finally attempting to hire him that morning. Despite her efforts to thoroughly check his background, there were secrets in Gideon's past. Three years ago he had resigned from the police department, and Colleen found herself wondering why a highly decorated officer would suddenly decide to quit and live like a reprobate on a run-down houseboat.

Withdrawing another cinnamon twist from the bag, she realized she didn't care about the secrets in Gideon Graves's past, nor did she care where or how he lived. All she wanted from the man was his expertise in finding missing persons. She wanted him to find Sam.

She got up off the sofa and went into her bedroom, where she quickly changed out of her work clothes and into a pair of jogging pants and a matching sweatshirt.

More comfortable, she went to the sofa and grabbed another cinnamon knot. With the sticky sweet pastry in one hand and the phone number on her lap, she picked up the phone and dialed Graves's number. It had rung only once when a soft knock fell on her door. "Come on in," Colleen yelled, assuming it was Elda, who often came over for an evening cup of tea.

The door flew open, and she swallowed hard as Gideon walked in, his features twisted into a threatening thundercloud. "Oh," she squeaked and hung up the phone. "I was just trying to call you." She stood up, refusing to be daunted by the fact that he seemed to fill the small living room with the width of his shoulders. His eyes glittered with what appeared to be suppressed anger.

He threw the folder she'd given him on the sofa. "I can only assume you were calling to tell me you'd mistakenly left out some information when you spoke to me this morning. Unimportant information like the fact that Sam Baker is wanted for murder."

"He didn't do it," she replied. "It's all a horrible mistake. He couldn't possibly have done it. I know Sam, and he could never murder anyone."

Gideon chuckled, a distinctly unpleasant sound. "He'll cheat on his wife and child, but he draws the line at murder?"

As he crossed the room and sank down on the sofa, Colleen breathed a small sigh of relief. Okay, so he'd discovered part of the truth, but apparently not all of it. He still believed she was Sam's lover, not his sister.

"I suppose his wife didn't understand him, and that's why he had to cheat on her. Perhaps his father didn't understand him, and that's why he had to kill him."

"That's ridiculous," Colleen scoffed. She sat down next to him on the sofa, far enough away so they didn't touch but close enough to smell him. He smelled like a salty breeze, and fresh sunshine, and the slight musk of male. "Look, I'm sorry I didn't tell you everything, but I was afraid you wouldn't take the case if you knew he was wanted for murder."

"I hate liars."

A heated flush crept up her neck, warming her cheeks. "I didn't lie. I just didn't tell."

"A lie of omission." He leaned back and raked a hand through his unruly hair. "What smells so good?"

Colleen pointed to the bag on the coffee table. "Cinnamon knots. My neighbor bakes them for me. Want one?" she offered grudgingly.

"Sure. I didn't have a chance to eat all day." He reached into the bag and withdrew one. "Got any coffee?"

"Are you going to take the case?"

He looked at her in surprise, and she noted for the first time that his eyes weren't really black. They were gray, with tiny flecks of gold around the pupils. They would be nice eyes if they weren't quite so fierce. "If I say no does that mean I have to eat this without any coffee?" he asked.

"If you say no I intend to grab that cinnamon knot out of your hand and eat it myself," she returned evenly.

He stared at her another moment, then laughed. This time it was a pleasant sound that shot through her with warmth even though she suspected he was laughing at her. His laughter did something pleasing to his features, alleviated the darkness, relaxed the taut lines and transformed him from disturbing to devastating. "Now that's the kind of honesty I can admire."

She raised her chin, meeting his gaze boldly. "I don't care much whether you admire me or not. I want to know if you're going to help me find Sam."

For the second time since meeting her, Gideon felt a flare of envy for Sam Baker. Colleen Jensen appeared single-minded in her desire to find the man. Gideon knew if he disappeared off the face of the earth tomorrow, nobody would grieve his absence, nobody would mourn his disappearance. Except perhaps Fast Eddy, and that, in itself, was a depressing thought. "I'm still considering if I should take the case or not."

She eyed him speculatively, then emitted a tiny sigh of exasperation. "And I suppose you could consider better if you had a cup of coffee?"

He grinned and looked at the cinnamon knot he still held in his fingers. "I believe I could." He watched as she left the living room, disappearing into what he assumed was the kitchen.

The moment she was gone, he looked around with interest. Gideon had learned early in his police training that observation of a person's living space often provided important clues to personality. And Gideon rarely took a case where he didn't know something about the person hiring him.

He probably could have discovered something about Colleen Jensen by checking motor vehicle information or records at the courthouse. But Gideon knew that would only provide him rudimentary dry material that would have little to do with the real Colleen Jensen. He preferred to rely on his own intuitive abilities and observation skills.

She liked nice things. That was the first thing he noticed when he looked around. The furniture was expensive, name brands that came with lifetime guarantees. He wondered what Sam had bought and paid for.

She also appeared to be obsessively neat. A place for everything and everything in its place. He looked at the coffee table, where pieces of sugar glaze had fallen off the cinnamon knot, looking like flakes of dandruff against the rich, dark wood. Perverse pleasure battled with guilt as he stared at the mess.

"Here we are," she said briskly as she reentered the room, carrying a tray with two cups of coffee and cream and sugar. He nodded as she handed him one of the cups.

Settling against the cushions of the sofa, he looked at her once again. There was no denying that she was an attractive woman. Even in the casual clothing, there was a grace to her movements, a natural elegance. The peach-colored sweat suit gave her cheeks a healthy glow and offset dramatically her dark curls. It was her eyes that captivated him, bewitching eyes, blue with just a touch of smoke.

He frowned. How he would love a cigarette. Well, he'd reached a decision. He would drink the coffee, eat the donut, then tell her he wasn't going to help her. The last thing he needed in his life was a case where the police were involved and the man was suspected of killing his father.

"Nice place you've got here," he observed. "Looks like you live pretty well on a social worker's salary."

She shrugged. "I get by."

With a little help from Sam Baker, Gideon guessed. Funny, she didn't look like his idea of a kept woman. But then Gideon was smart enough to know not to judge a book by its cover.

Still, there was something appealingly innocent about her. A lack of guile in her eyes, a candor Gideon found disconcerting. He frowned and popped the last of the cinnamon knot into his mouth. Time to tell the lady no and get the hell out of here. He drained the coffee and stood up. She rose, as well, a tiny frown line appearing between her eyebrows.

"Look, Ms. Jensen," he began.

"Colleen. If we're going to be working together please call me Colleen." Her voice radiated with an underlying desperation, and for the first time in years Gideon felt like a heel. It was not a pleasant feeling.

"That's just it. We aren't going to be working together." He paused at the door, refusing to be drawn into the deep disappointment that darkened her eyes.

"But you ate my cinnamon knot," she said, as if somehow in doing so he had made a solemn vow.

"Sam is wanted for murder. He's being sought by the police. He's been gone for months. Don't you think if he wanted to be in touch with you, somehow he would have gotten through by now?"

She moved to stand next to him, bringing with her the sweet scent of her floral perfume. She placed a hand on his arm. Her fingertips barely pressed into his skin, but he felt the touch as if it contained fire.

"This is something I have to do," she said. "I can't just sit and wait. I have to know if he's okay. I need to know that he's not—" She broke off and stepped away from him. When she turned around her eyes radiated unexpected strength, steely determination. "Mr. Graves, I intend to follow through in hiring a private detective. I've heard you're the best. But if I can't get you to take the case, then I'll settle for second-best."

Gideon frowned, once again getting the overwhelming feeling that his life was out of control. There were a thousand reasons he shouldn't take this case. And only one reason he was going to. He knew if he didn't, her eyes would haunt him forever. And he was haunted enough already.

"Two weeks," he reluctantly relented. "I'll give you two weeks, and if I don't come up with any fresh leads or clues to Sam's whereabouts, then that will be the end of it as far as I'm concerned."

She nodded. "Thank you."

"Don't thank me. I haven't done anything yet." He opened the door, then turned to her one last time. "There aren't any other little surprises you've forgotten to mention to me, are there?"

"Of course not," she answered after a beat of hesitation. Her gaze met his, unflinching. She was either being completely honest, or she was one hell of a liar.

As he walked down the sidewalk toward his car, he wondered why he was so certain it was the latter.

Chapter Three

"Hi, Gideon." Fast Eddy greeted him as he walked out of his houseboat the next morning.

Gideon stifled a groan. Hadn't the boy gone home at all last night? Eddy had been waiting for him when he'd gotten home the night before, eager to show off the cleaning he'd done during Gideon's absence. In truth, Gideon had been surprised at what Eddy had managed to accomplish. The living quarters sparkled with a cleanliness they hadn't enjoyed in the three years he had been living there.

"I was just on my way out," Gideon said, fighting against a wave of guilt.

"Oh." The smile on Eddy's face slipped just a notch. "Working on the case?"

"Actually, I was just on my way to the Harbor for some breakfast." Gideon paused a moment, wondering what it was about Eddy that touched him. "Have you had breakfast?" he asked.

Eddy shook his head.

"Come on, I'll buy you some eggs, and we'll talk about what kind of work you'll be doing for me."

"Sure, that sounds great," Eddy exclaimed, his voice squeaking with ill-concealed excitement.

As they walked toward the restaurant, Gideon was aware of Eddy mimicking his walk, making his strides mirror Gideon's. Gideon immediately regretted his impulse, knowing there was no way now he could take back the offer of breakfast or work.

What was it about this fresh-faced, red-haired kid that managed to push all his buttons? He didn't consider himself a compassionate man, but something about Eddy managed to burst through his defenses and find a core of empathy.

The Harbor Restaurant was a popular place for breakfast among the fishermen in the area. When Gideon and Eddy walked in, the early morning eaters had already come and gone, leaving the two their pick of tables.

Gideon chose a booth in the back, the same place he ate breakfast most mornings.

"I know why you sit back here," Eddy said as he slid in across from Gideon. "Private eyes always sit in the back of places so they can see if trouble walks in the front door." He looked at Gideon proudly.

Gideon sighed inwardly, not having the heart to tell Eddy that the only reason he sat back here was that he was close enough to the coffeepot to pour his own when the waitress was too busy.

"So, did you take the dame's case?" Eddy asked as soon as the waitress had taken their orders and disappeared into the kitchen.

"Temporarily." Gideon frowned, his thoughts reluctantly pulled back to Colleen Jensen. She'd occupied his dreams last night. Although he had not been able to remember exactly what he'd dreamed, he'd awakened knowing she'd been a central ingredient in a restless night.

"What's her story?"

"She wants me to find a friend of hers." Eddy's eager smile once again wavered, and Gideon knew the kid had been hoping for something juicier than a missing friend case. "Her friend is wanted by the police. He's the main suspect in a murder case."

Eddy's eyes widened and his Adam's apple bobbed as he swallowed convulsively. "Wow." He leaned across the table. "Sounds like a two-man case. You gonna let me help you with this one?"

Gideon considered Eddy's comment for a long moment. The kid had delusions of grandeur concerning the life of a private detective. He expected a life of fancy cars, fast women and danger, and nothing was further from the truth. "Okay Eddy, for the next couple of weeks you can consider yourself my partner." He named the figure he would pay per hour, unsurprised when Eddy protested he didn't need to be paid.

"Heck, if I had any money, I'd pay you," Eddy exclaimed, his blue eyes shining bright with excitement.

Their conversation was interrupted by the appearance of the waitress with their food. As they ate, Gideon was thankful that Eddy seemed occupied with his thoughts, for a change not filling the silence with idle chatter.

Gideon ate slowly, mechanically, his thoughts on the case he had agreed to take. Thankfully, with modern technology, much of his search for Sam Baker would take place via his computer. Colleen had provided him the man's social security number and his driver's license number. It was a starting place. However, Gideon knew before he began his search in earnest he would need to ask Colleen Jensen some in-depth questions about her lover.

"Gideon, is everything all right?"

He started and realized for a moment he'd forgotten Eddy's presence. "Sure. Why?"

"You were really scowling." Eddy looked at him anxiously. "You aren't going to change your mind about hiring me, are you?"

"No, Eddy, I was just thinking about the case."

Eddy nodded and popped the last of a piece of toast into his mouth. "The case of the gorgeous dame and her deadly friend," he said as he chewed. "It would make a great movie of the week."

"Only if we solve it," Gideon replied dryly. He finished his coffee, then stood up. He dug into his pocket and withdrew enough money to pay for the meal. Throwing it on the table, he waited for Eddy to drain his glass of milk, then together they left the restaurant and stepped out into the autumn sunshine.

"So, where do we begin to crack this case wide open?" Eddy asked enthusiastically.

Gideon pulled a twenty-dollar bill out of his pocket and handed it to Eddy. "I want you to go to the library and photocopy every newspaper article you can find concerning the death of Joseph Baker."

Eddy's face fell. Although he didn't grumble or voice a single complaint, Gideon knew this sort of library drudgery wasn't exactly the kind of glamorous detective work he'd had in mind. Tough. The kid might as well understand the reality of being a detective, which rarely involved fast cars, beautiful women and danger.

"You might also cross-reference and copy anything you can find on Baker Enterprises and the family," Gideon continued. "Then I'll meet you at the houseboat some time this afternoon."

"Okay. Don't worry, I'll get a copy of everything that's ever been printed on the Bakers," Eddy promised. "When Fast Eddy does a job, he does it right." He started to leave, but paused when Gideon called his name.

"Wipe your mouth, Eddy," he instructed. He mentally groaned. He had a case he wasn't sure he wanted and a new partner who sported a milk mustache. How could things possibly get any worse?

Moments later he parked his car along Bay Shore's Main Street, in front of the tiny office that announced the building to be Suffolk County Social Services. For a long minute he simply sat in the car, dreading the thought of going inside and speaking with Colleen.

He should have asked her all the questions he needed to the night before. However, the moment she had touched him, the instant her fingers had lingered on his arm, he only knew the need to escape. He scoffed now, realizing his reaction to her had probably been an odd, residual effect of his hangover combined with his irritation over her misrepresentation of the facts of Sam's disappearance.

Getting out of the car, he supposed he should be grateful that at least she hadn't lied about where she lived or worked. He could even forgive her lie of omission, understanding her fear that the murder might keep him from taking the case.

He walked into the office, unsurprised to find the small space filled with women and children. The receptionist looked harassed and exhausted despite the fact that it was only a few minutes after ten. "May I help you?" she asked as he approached.

"I need to speak with Colleen Jensen," he said, then jumped in surprise as somebody grabbed him around the knee. He looked down into the grinning, drooling face of a toddler who gripped his leg to steady his wobbly, chubby legs.

"Do you have an appointment?" the receptionist asked. The phone rang and she answered it, holding up a hand to Gideon. "Do you have an appointment?" she repeated when she hung up the phone.

"Uh, no, but I'm sure she'll want to see me."

"Name?"

"Bond...James Bond," he answered with a cheeky grin. The receptionist obviously had no sense of humor. "Gideon Graves," he added as she glared at him balefully.

"Have a seat, and I'll let you know when she's available."

Gideon stood uncertainly, afraid to take a step and topple the toddler, who laced a string of drool from his knee to his ankle. Helplessly, he eyed the women, seeking the mother of the kid, but it was difficult to tell which of the dozen children belonged to which mother.

He finally picked up the child, found an empty chair, then sat down and placed the kid on the floor in front of him. The little boy giggled, then crawled over to a woman reading a magazine.

For a moment Gideon watched the child as he pulled himself up using his mother's knees. He looked at Gideon and laughed again, as if inordinately pleased with himself.

A piercing ache of banished dreams ripped through Gideon. He'd wanted children once, had hoped to build a family of laughing, happy offspring. However, like so many of his dreams, that one had also been stolen by Anne. Anne and her money.

He frowned, shoving aside old memories, ancient bitterness. Instead he looked at his wristwatch, wondering how long he would have to wait before speaking with Colleen.

It was a little over an hour later when his name was finally called and the receptionist showed him into Colleen's tiny office. Twice in that hour she'd stuck her head out of the office, appealing for him to be patient.

As he entered, she stood up, looking as frazzled, as tired as the receptionist had looked. "A person could grow old waiting to get in to see you," Gideon said with a touch of irritation.

"I apologize. It's been a full schedule today, and I really didn't think it was fair to see you before the clients who had appointments." She motioned to the chair in front of her desk. "Please, sit down."

Gideon frowned. The office was far too small and filled with the lovely scent of her perfume. "It's after eleven. How about we go someplace and grab a sandwich?" At least in a café or diner he would smell hot grease and sizzling meat instead of the mind-muddying fragrance of her.

"I usually don't go to lunch..." She looked at her appointment schedule. "I suppose I could take forty minutes or so." She grabbed her purse and together they left the office and walked out to the sidewalk.

"There's a diner on the next block. That okay?" he asked.

She nodded. "When I get a chance to have lunch, that's usually where I go."

"You always have mornings as busy as this one?" he asked curiously.

"I'd love to be able to say no, but unfortunately it was pretty typical of most mornings." She smiled and shook her head. "We're accustomed to functioning in an atmosphere that borders chaos."

"You like your work," he observed.

Her smile was full and warm. "I can't imagine doing anything else for a living. There's something very rewarding in knowing you're making a difference in people's lives, fighting hopelessness, alleviating despair." She blushed, as if embarrassed by her zeal, and shook her head, causing her curls to dance impishly in the bright sunshine. "Sorry, I tend to be a bore when it comes to my love of my work."

"There's nothing boorish about liking what you do," Gideon returned. "I find that a rather admirable trait." She blushed again, and Gideon found himself wondering how on earth a young woman who blushed so easily had ever gotten herself involved in an affair with Sam Baker.

"What about you? Do you like your work?" she asked.

He shrugged. "It's all right," he replied, grateful they'd reached the diner and no further answer seemed anticipated. It was a question he rarely asked himself.

It wasn't until they'd placed their orders and the waitress had departed that Colleen looked at him expectantly. "I assume there's a reason for this meeting?"

He withdrew a small notepad and a pen from his shirt pocket. "In order to find Sam, I need a little more information about him."

She frowned and again he sensed secrets in the depths of her smoky eyes.

"What kind of information?" She averted her gaze from his and instead looked at the place mat.

"What did Sam like to do in his spare time? Did he have hobbies? Close friends? Was there anyone who might have aided him in his disappearance?"

Her frown deepened, creating a small furrow in the center of her forehead. Gideon fought the impulse to reach across the table and rub away the crease. Her skin looked so soft, so touchable. Instead he wrapped his hands around his water glass, irritated by his wayward thoughts.

"Sam didn't have hobbies," she answered, finally looking at him once again. "And he didn't really have close friends. He was kind of a workaholic." She looked at her hands laced together on the tabletop, then at Gideon. "I hate this," she said softly, her voice filled with emotion. "I'm talking about him in the past tense . . . like he's dead."

"He might be." Gideon didn't say it to be unkind, but he also didn't want to give her any false hope. Three months was a long time for a man to be on the run. Anything was possible. "Or he might just be very good at staying hidden," he added, compelled to say something to reduce the grief that darkened her eyes.

Their conversation halted long enough for the waitress to serve them. "Did Sam ever mention any place he'd like to visit?" Sam asked the moment the waitress had departed. "Was there a city, a state... a country he ever mentioned?"

She shook her head. "Sam was satisfied with his life in the here and now. He never wanted to be anywhere else but with his family and working."

"And with you," Gideon added.

"Of course," she replied quickly. She focused on her hamburger, meticulously picking off the onions before cutting it in half.

"Don't like onions?"

"I love them." She smiled. "But I'll be spending the rest of the afternoon talking with clients in a very small office."

Gideon reached over and took the onions on the side of her plate and added them to his hamburger. "I love them, and I don't much care if my breath is offensive."

"Somehow, that doesn't surprise me," she observed with a small grin.

He looked at her in surprise. "What's that supposed to mean?"

Her smile lingered as she shrugged. "I just imagine you're the kind of man who finds pleasure in being perverse."

"And what has caused you to think that?"

"You ate my cinnamon knot last night knowing full well you intended to tell me you weren't going to take the case."

Gideon laughed. "Guilty as charged," he confessed, then sobered. "But I vindicated myself by changing my mind and taking your case."

She tilted her head and gazed at him curiously. "What did make you decide to change your mind?"

There was no way Gideon could answer her truthfully. He couldn't tell her he'd decided to take the case solely because of the emotional impact of her eyes. "Boredom," he finally answered. "Besides, I never turn down a healthy fee," he finished flatly, not wanting to invite any further personal questions from her.

He suddenly realized he was beginning to like her, and it unsettled him. It had been a very long time since Gideon had liked anyone. He'd promised himself three years ago that he'd never care about anyone again. And he positively could not allow himself to feel anything for a client, particularly this one, who was obviously deeply, desperately in love with a missing man.

Colleen immediately knew in some way she'd stepped over some personal boundary with her innocent question. She could tell in the way his features tightened, his eyes darkened and he focused on his meal. He'd withdrawn completely and totally, like a perverse flower closing its leaves to the warmth of the sun.

No problem, she thought with a flicker of irritation. It had been an innocent enough question on her part. In truth, she didn't much care why he'd decided to take the case. She just wanted him to find out if Sam was all right. That's all she wanted from Gideon Graves.

As they finished eating in silence, she cast surreptitious gazes at him, finding him a fascinating bundle of contradictions. He emitted the aura of unbendable strength, of self-containment, and yet something about him, some elusive quality hinted at a vulnerability deep inside him.

His hair was unruly, as if it hadn't received the benefit of a comb for days, and yet it shone with cleanliness. His posture appeared relaxed, but on closer inspection she noted a subtle tenseness, a studied watchfulness that betrayed his image of relaxation.

Yes, an interesting bundle of contradictions. She flushed as his eyes met hers and a spark of unexpected warmth shot through her. Confused and surprised, she quickly broke the gaze and once again focused on her lunch.

She was relieved when he began asking her more questions about Sam, although they were questions she felt helplessly inadequate to answer. For a moment she wondered if the best thing to do was to come completely clean, confess that Sam wasn't her lover, but instead was her brother.

She bit her tongue, refusing to give in to the impulse. That information was what had messed things up with the last three detectives. Besides, if he was really as good as he professed to be, he'd eventually discover her true relationship with Sam, but she hoped not before he'd gained the information she so desperately desired.

"So when can I expect to hear something from you?" she asked as they walked to her office. She tried to ignore the way the sunlight stroked glistening highlights in his dark hair, the self-assured strides of his long legs, all the little personal nuances that merely added to his attractiveness.

"I should have some kind of a preliminary report in a couple of days."

She nodded as they stopped walking and paused in front of her office building. "You'll call me?"

"As soon as I have something to report." He hesitated a moment, looking at her as if she somehow held the last piece to a complex puzzle. "Tell me something, Colleen. You're obviously an attractive, bright young woman. What did you hope to gain by your relationship with Sam Baker?"

"What did I hope to gain?" She frowned thoughtfully, her gaze locked with his. "I just loved him." When he looked at her skeptically, she continued, "Mr. Graves, my love doesn't come with a price tag. I give it as a gift, expecting nothing in return."

He laughed, the unpleasant sound discordant with heavy cynicism. "I can't figure you out. You're either an accomplished liar or a naive fool.'' Without waiting for her response, he turned and walked away.

Colleen watched him, noting how his shirt pulled taut across the width of his shoulders and the way his tight jeans hugged his slender hips. He was definitely a sexy enigma. Just before he'd turned to walk away, Colleen had seen a glimpse of that elusive vulnerability in his eyes. It had been fleeting, but compelling.

She'd spent the past two years since her divorce steering clear of men, especially ones like Gideon Graves. Her husband had been handsome to a fault, with that edge of simmering emotions that hinted at dangerous intensity. Heartbreakers. Her experience with her ex-husband had taught her to steer clear of that particular variety of man.

She knew better than anyone that love often came with a price tag, but she had quickly learned her husband's price was far too high.

Frowning, she wondered what price Gideon had once paid. Whatever it had been, from his scornful smirks it had apparently also been too high. Or perhaps he simply believed her to be a bloodsucking mistress only interested in the expensive pretties her wealthy lover could buy her. He'd said she was either a liar or a fool for loving without demanding a price. Perhaps she was a little of both.

What bothered her most was why she cared at all what Gideon thought of her. All she wanted from him was his expertise in finding out something about Sam. He would be in her life two weeks. She would pay him, then he would be gone. She would get what she wanted, information about Sam. And he would get what he wanted, a generous fee. An easy business transaction, nothing more, nothing less.

As she turned to go into the building, she wondered why she had the sinking feeling that nothing was going to work out quite as easily as she hoped.

Chapter Four

Eddy was waiting for Gideon when he finally returned to the houseboat that afternoon. The skinny kid jumped from the plastic lounger on the deck, his face lighting up as Gideon approached.

"Gideon, you won't believe how much stuff I found at the library on the Baker case," he exclaimed, and pointed to a stack of papers on the deck at his feet.

"Bring them inside and let's see what you've got." He unlocked the door and pushed it open, waiting as Eddy gathered the material, then Gideon followed him inside.

He grabbed a beer for himself and a soda for Eddy from the refrigerator, then joined the kid at the table where he had laid out the copies he'd made at the library.

"This was a big murder case, Gideon," Eddy explained, his face radiating excitement.

"Murder is always big," Gideon observed absently as he popped the tab on his beer can and took a deep swallow, trying to shove lingering thoughts of Colleen Jensen out of his mind.

After he'd left her, he'd spent the rest of the afternoon taking care of the errands necessary in the daily routine of living. He'd taken a pile of clothes to the Laundromat that washed and folded, he'd paid another two months of berth space for the houseboat, and he'd chased down a client who owed him a final check for services rendered. And the whole time he'd been doing these mundane errands, his head had been filled with Colleen.

Somehow, someway, something about Colleen Jensen had managed to crawl beneath the defenses he'd erected over the three years since his divorce.

It couldn't be that Colleen reminded him of the woman he had once loved. Physically Colleen and Anne were nothing alike. Anne had been a cool blonde, tall and willowy. Colleen was short, petite, and her dark hair and blue-gray eyes emitted vitality and an earthiness Anne had lacked. So what was it about Colleen Jensen that affected him so strongly?

He normally prided himself on being a fairly good judge of character. He'd only been fooled completely once, and that had been by Anne. For the life of him, he couldn't get a handle on Colleen Jensen.

He didn't know whether to believe that she was an innocent victim, a nice social worker who been taken advantage of by a wealthy, unscrupulous man, or a smart seductress who slept with Sam Baker to feather her nest with things she couldn't otherwise afford.

He tried to focus on the paperwork in front of him. He'd quit reading papers and watching the news a long time ago, when he'd found himself the subject of headlines. Seeing his own story twisted and turned by the media had bred in him an enormous mistrust of the press. Unfortunately, short of seeing the actual police records of the crime, the news articles were his only access to information.

"It looks really bad for this Sam Baker guy," Eddy said as he studied one of the papers. "It says here that a security guard at Baker Enterprises saw him running from the building minutes before Joseph Baker was discovered dead."

"Yeah, it doesn't look good," Gideon agreed. As he read article after article on Joseph Baker's murder and the subsequent disappearance of Sam Baker, he tried not to feel pity for Colleen. All the evidence pointed to Sam's culpability, and even if the man was innocent, with so much evidence against him the odds were good that if he was found he'd probably spend the rest of his life in jail.

"At first I couldn't find anything written up on the Baker family," Eddy explained as Gideon scanned page after page. "Although Joseph Baker made the financial news regularly. I finally decided to check the society pages and see if I could find anything there. On the bottom of the stack are photocopies of all the mentions the Baker family got in the society columns."

"Good work," Gideon said, causing Eddy to beam with pride. "That's it for today, Eddy. You can go on home," he said, knowing it would take him some time to read through all the material, and that nothing more would be accomplished until he'd read everything.

"You sure there's nothing else I can do for you? I mean, I don't have to be home at any special time."

Again Gideon felt a curious empathy for the kid. He knew Eddy's father was a truck driver and his mother spent most of her evenings in a local tavern, rarely sober by the time she stumbled home.

Yes, Gideon knew all about lonely nights. His life had been filled with them. Still, he was nobody's keeper and refused to take on the responsibility of being Eddy's hero.

"Go on home, Eddy. I'll have something for you to do in the morning." He hardened himself against the yearning in Eddy's eyes. Instead he focused his gaze on the papers before him.

"Okay, good night, Gideon," Eddy said softly as he walked out the door. When he was gone, Gideon reared back in his chair and took another deep swallow from his beer can.

Sooner or later Eddy would realize Gideon was nobody to hang a hero hat on. Somewhere along the line the kid would hear the stories surrounding Gideon's resignation from the police force. He would hear the tales of the fallen angel and eventually he would leave, just like everyone else in Gideon's life.

He thought again of Colleen and the deep burning in her eyes when she spoke of her love for Sam. Gideon wondered what it felt like to be loved so deeply, so completely. He'd thought he'd been loved like that once . . . with Anne. But her love had been a lie. He wondered if Colleen's was a lie, as well.

For just a moment he remembered the sweet scent of Colleen's perfume, the warmth of her smile as she'd sat across the table from him in the diner. He'd been irritated at having to wait so long in her office before she saw him, but knew he would have been even more irritated had she ushered him right in ahead of the clients who needed her help. Again he found himself wondering about the dynamics in her relationship to Sam. Had the wealthy entrepreneur taken advantage of her innocence and turned her sensible head with expensive gifts? Or had the sexy social worker set her sights on the rich Sam Baker with the relentlessness of a predator?

He drained the beer can and crushed it, angry at himself and his thoughts. He had work to do. Why was he wasting time wondering about such nonsense as love and Colleen Jensen? Drawing his attention to the papers, he shoved all other thoughts out of his mind.

He'd been reading and taking notes for about an hour when he picked up one of the photocopies on the bottom of the pile. It was from the society pages. A grainy picture of Joseph Baker and his four children attending a charity ball. A handsome family, he thought as he focused on the son. Sam. Tall, with dark hair and strong features, Sam Baker was a handsome young man.

Gideon's gaze shifted to his sisters, Carolyn, Bonnie and Colleen. The blood drained from his face as he stared at the image of Colleen Baker. The heart-shaped face, the curly dark hair, the smiling eyes... there was absolutely no mistake. Colleen Jensen wasn't Sam Baker's lover. She was his sister.

The front legs of his chair slammed to the floor with a bang as he continued to stare at the photo of Colleen Jensen Baker. Why had she lied? God, he felt like such a fool. He'd spent so much time wondering if Colleen was a possible gold digger, and all the time she'd owned the mine.

What in the hell was going on beneath those pretty curls atop her head? Why in the hell had she lied? He grabbed his car keys from the table. That's just what he intended to find out.

It took him only minutes to drive to Colleen's duplex. He was disappointed to find her car not there. No problem. He would wait. As long as it took, he would be there when she got home.

Pulling a stick of licorice from the package in the glove box, he stared at the modest home. Red brick with painted shutters to match, the duplex was attractive but certainly nothing special.

Why was Colleen Baker living here in this unassuming duplex when she could afford anything she wanted? Why the job as a social worker when she probably had enough money to last if she didn't work a day for the rest of her life? Was this some sort of a game? Princess playing pauper for a while? And where exactly did *he* fit into this charade?

"I'm about to find out," he murmured as he spied her car pulling into the driveway behind him. He threw the last of the licorice stick out the window, then got out of his car, self-righteous anger propelling him toward her. And to think he'd felt guilty about charging the poor little social worker his usual fee.

"What a surprise," she said as she got out of her car. "You have something for me already?" She looked at him hopefully.

For a moment Gideon's anger was swept away beneath the beauty of the vision of the setting sun painting her features in vibrant golden tones. She'd shed the suit jacket she'd worn earlier in the day, giving him full view of the thrust of her breasts against the feminine white blouse. An ember of heat uncoiled in his stomach, reigniting the anger that had brought him here. "We need to talk." He gestured toward the house.

"Maybe we should talk right here," she said, eyeing him uncomfortably. She shifted from foot to foot, obviously aware of his anger.

"No problem. I can quit this assignment just as easily out here as I can inside, Ms. Baker."

Her eyes flared at the name, then filled with a weary resignation. She threaded her fingers through her hair, causing the curls to dance provocatively. "I guess we'd better go inside," she said and slammed her car door. "If my blood is about to be spilled, I don't want it ruining Elda's flowers."

He had to hand it to her, she'd lied, she'd been caught, but she obviously wasn't ashamed. "I think you owe me an explanation," he said.

"I do." She leaned against her car door, suddenly looking tired. "And I suppose you'll reconsider the case if I agree to a bigger fee. Isn't that the way it works?" There was a touch of bitterness in her tone. "You initially gave me the fee for an ordinary person, but now that you know I'm a Baker, and worth a lot of money, the fee becomes higher?"

He looked at her in surprise. "Is that what you've experienced?"

She nodded. "With three different private investigators. They quoted me a fee, then as our conversation continued and they realized I was a Baker, the price suddenly tripled." She smiled humorlessly. "I decided to try a different approach with you."

"Did you really believe I wouldn't find out?" Gideon asked.

"I figured you'd find out sooner or later. I just hoped it would be later." She shoved away from the car and motioned for him to follow her. "Come on in. Perhaps I can work up the energy to apologize over a cup of coffee."

He followed her to the front door, wondering how she had managed to make him feel like he was the one who needed to apologize on behalf of his profession. How had she managed so easily to defuse his anger?

She unlocked the front door and pushed it open. She took a step inside, then stopped abruptly, causing Gideon to bump hard into her back. "Oh, God," she said softly.

"What? What's wrong?" Gideon asked.

"Somebody has been here." She stepped aside and sagged against the doorframe, allowing Gideon to move around her.

The living room was in shambles. Books had been pulled from shelves, couch cushions thrown from the sofa, the contents of the desk drawers had been emptied onto the floor. "Stay here," Gideon commanded.

It took him only minutes to check the other rooms and discern the intruder was no longer in the duplex. Whoever had wreaked the havoc was gone. He returned to where Colleen still stood at the door, apparently frozen by the scene before her.

He touched her arm softly. "You'd better call the police."

"Would you do it for me? I...I don't feel very well." She stumbled to a rocking chair and sank down into it, her gaze skipping and jumping around the room in stunned disbelief.

Gideon nodded and picked up the phone. It took him only a moment to call the appropriate station and report the break-in. The officer taking the report promised a responding unit would be by as soon as possible.

Gideon frowned as he hung up the receiver. He could have sworn he heard several clicks that didn't belong on the line.

"Are they sending somebody?" Colleen asked.

He looked at her sympathetically, noting the paleness of her face, the slight tremble of her hand as she pushed an errant strand of her hair from her forehead. From years of police work, he knew well the shock, the horror, the feelings of violation that accompanied a break-in. "Officers should be here soon."

He walked around the living room, careful not to touch anything, but assessing, cataloguing his impressions. "Can you tell by just looking around if anything is missing?" he asked.

Her gaze moved slowly around the room, and he noted that the color was returning to her face. "No...nothing seems to be missing." She frowned and looked at him. "This isn't an ordinary burglary, is it? I mean, whoever broke in here left the television, the VCR and the stereo unit. If it was just a robbery, wouldn't those things be gone?"

"It looks to me like somebody was searching for something," Gideon said thoughtfully.

"But what could anyone be looking for?" she asked.

He smiled ruefully. "I was kind of hoping you'd know the answer to that." He could see she was still deeply shaken. "You didn't somehow orchestrate this because you knew I was coming over to yell at you, did you?"

She smiled. It wasn't a full smile, but it was enough to assure Gideon that she was really all right. "I have a feeling this has only postponed your yelling at me."

He didn't have a chance to reply, for at that moment officers appeared at the door.

The next couple of hours were a blur for Colleen. First there was the horror of walking in on the scene, followed by questions from the police. More than anything there was a palpable tension between Gideon and the responding officers, a tension she didn't understand.

She was almost relieved when the officers finished their report and left, although there remained a horrifying fear as she surveyed her violated home.

This had been her nest, her personal piece of the earth where she felt safe and secure, surrounded by the things she loved. Now the peace and the serenity were tainted, destroyed.

"I can't believe this was done by wayward kids," she said, repeating what the police officers had suspected as she placed books on the shelves.

"I agree," Gideon replied, his expression grim as he put the cushions on the sofa, then sat down. "Look, it's going to take you all night to get this place in shape so you can sleep, and you're already exhausted. Why don't you stay at my houseboat for the night, then take the day tomorrow to clean up here?"

Colleen hesitated. The idea of staying at Gideon's place wasn't particularly appealing, but she definitely liked it better than remaining here for the rest of the night. She knew sleep would be impossible if she stayed here. The knowledge that somebody had easily picked the lock of her back door once this evening and could just as easily do it again would keep sleep at bay.

She would feel safer at Gideon's, and at the moment that's all she wanted. Besides, he was right. She was exhausted. "I'll just get a few things together." She went into the bedroom, where her dresser drawers had been emptied onto the bed and the contents of her jewelry box were scattered in the middle of the bedspread.

As she packed a bag, she wondered for the hundredth time who had been here, looking through her things, seeking something specific.

When she came out of the bedroom, Gideon was waiting by the front door, his face an inscrutable mask. "Ready?"

She nodded, wondering briefly if she was making a mistake. She really knew nothing about Gideon, but oddly enough she trusted him. "You aren't going to yell at me tonight, are you?" she asked, suddenly remembering what had brought him to her house in the first place.

A whisper of a smile curved his lips. "I think I can hold off until tomorrow, but there are some more questions I'd like to ask you."

A few minutes later Colleen sat in the passenger side of Gideon's car. They had decided to leave Colleen's car parked in the driveway. Gideon promised he would take her to work the next morning, then home afterward. She had insisted she couldn't take the day off, knew there were just too many people who depended on her being in the office.

"Before you go back to your place tomorrow, I want a friend of mine to go in and sweep it for bugs," Gideon said as they drove toward the marina.

Colleen stared at him in surprise. "I don't have a bug problem. Maybe an occasional spider."

He laughed. "Not that kind of bug. Electronic equipment, listening devices. When I used your phone I heard something that sounded like a wiretap."

"You're kidding! Why on earth would anyone want to spy on me?"

"I was hoping you could answer that." He cast her a sardonic look. "Maybe you have a few more little secrets you've forgotten to mention?"

Colleen flushed. "You promised you wouldn't yell tonight."

"I'm not yelling, I'm merely asking," he countered. "If I'm going to help you figure this all out, I need to know everything."

"I've told you everything," Colleen replied. "Well, maybe not quite everything," she added. She jumped as Gideon muttered an oath and slammed the palm of his hand against the steering wheel.

"Hand me a stick of licorice out of the glove box," he commanded. "Antismoking therapy," he explained as he took the candy from her and stuck it into the side of his mouth. "Now, tell me everything that you've left out."

Colleen sighed. "I've just had the feeling since Sam disappeared that I'm being watched, followed." She frowned and rubbed her forehead thoughtfully. "At first I figured it was the police. They know Sam and I are close, and maybe they assumed he'd contact me in some way." She shivered, remembering those days and weeks following her father's death and Sam's disappearance.

"It's possible the police were watching you after the murder. But they don't have the manpower to continue that kind of surveillance for months on end, except perhaps on Sam's house."

She nodded. "I know they're still watching his house. Julienne, Sam's wife, told me." She hesitated a moment, staring at her hands folded in her lap. "I also think Sam was at my place last week." She winced as Gideon expelled another colorful curse.

"What makes you think so?" he finally asked, his fingers white as they gripped the steering wheel. She guessed he was probably imagining the wheel as her neck.

"Just a feeling. I got home from work and knew somebody had been in the house. Nothing had been disturbed, but I knew somebody had been there. I just had the feeling it might have been Sam. I thought I smelled his cologne. I know it sounds crazy." She drew in a shaky breath. "Now I'm not so sure. It could have been anyone."

"And you didn't think that was important enough to tell me?" He shook his head. "You people positively amaze me," he finally said, throwing the remainder of his licorice stick out the car window, as if she'd made the taste go bad.

"You people?"

"The rich, the elite, the ones who think the rules are made for everyone else." The rancor in his tone momentarily stole her breath away. "You manipulate people's lives, tell half-truths, write your own ticket to whatever serves your purpose." He drew in a deep breath and expelled it as a sigh. "I'm sorry. I'm out of line."

"Yes, you are," she agreed coolly. "You know nothing about me, and I resent your characterization. I haven't exactly gotten a great impression of private investigators, but I'm willing to withhold judgment on you for the time being."

"I told you before, I really don't care what you or anyone else thinks of me," he returned.

"That's probably the only sentiment we share," she replied.

For the remainder of the drive to the houseboat they didn't speak. It was a tense silence, filled with unanswered questions and the residual ashes of mistrust.

She glanced sideways, noting the taut line of his jaw, his tightly compressed lips. It was obvious he didn't trust her, and she couldn't blame him for that. She hadn't been exactly stellar in the truth department. But she'd had a lifetime of learning to protect herself when it came to her family background and status. The one time she'd let down her guard, her heart had been ripped in two.

She realized now she'd been foolish to think Gideon wouldn't find out she wasn't Sam's lover. She should have been truthful with him from the very beginning. The important thing was that he find Sam. Nothing else mattered. Not his opinion of her, and certainly not her opinion of him.

She started as the car came to a halt, then realized they had reached the marina. "I'll get your bag," he said as they got out of the car. He reached in the back seat and grabbed the small overnight suitcase she'd brought with her.

Following him down the ramp that led to his houseboat, Colleen wondered why she had so easily agreed to stay here for the night. Almost immediately the answer came to her. She was afraid. The possibility that somebody might be spying on her, watching her or eavesdropping on all her conversations filled her with horror. If it wasn't the police, then who? And what did they want from her?

No, there was no way she wanted to stay at her house for the night. A motel room held little appeal. She didn't want to be alone.

A sudden bitterness welled up in the back of her throat. She was a Baker, heiress to a fortune, and yet she was spending the night with a stranger, a man she wasn't even sure she liked, because she didn't want to be alone . . . and there was nobody else she could turn to.

"It's not exactly the Plaza, but it's home," Gideon said as he pushed open the door and ushered her inside.

"Looks like you've cleaned some since I was here," she observed, grateful that the interior smelled of pine cleaner and lemon polish rather than stale beer and old food.

"I'll just change the sheets on the bed," he said.

"Please, don't bother. I can sleep right here." She gestured to the sofa.

His dark eyebrows rose mockingly. "I wouldn't want you to think I'm not a gentleman."

"Too late. I knew you weren't a gentleman when you ate my cinnamon knot."

"Aren't you a little nervous about spending the night with a man who readily admits to being no gentleman?" He moved closer to her, bringing with him the distinctive scent she found so provocative.

She stepped back from him, her eyes widening as she realized again she knew nothing about this man. "Certainly I'm not nervous," she answered with a touch of bravado. She set her suitcase on the sofa. "I'm sure you realize if you don't act like a gentleman tonight, then you won't have my case to work on tomorrow.''

His gaze remained on her, dark and enigmatic. "Perhaps by tomorrow morning I won't want your case."

"This is a ridiculous conversation," Colleen finally said. She swiped a hand through her hair, exhausted and confused not only by the events of the night but by his vague innuendos, as well.

"Don't worry, Colleen," he finally said. "You're safe here. You'd be one of the last women on earth I'd choose to be ungentlemanly with."

"Why? Oh, I imagine as a dangerous private eye you prefer flashy, big-breasted blondes instead of intelligent, small-breasted brunettes." She flushed, appalled at her own words.

He paused in the doorway, his gaze lingering on her chest. He smiled. "No, I'd say your breasts are just right." His eyes moved to hers. "But I have an aversion to big wallets and powerful family names."

"Unless they're paying your fee?" Colleen said thinly.

"That's right," he answered without hesitation. "After all, a man's got to make a living. There's nothing I like better than taking a wealthy person's money. Good night, Colleen." He turned and left, closing his bedroom door behind him.

She hated him, Colleen decided as she went into the tiny bathroom to change into her pajamas. He was rude and arrogant and obnoxious.

When she left the bathroom she discovered a sheet and a blanket on the couch. Oh, she knew his type, all right. He wasn't about to drop the case and send her on her way. It was obvious he lived on the edge of poverty. He wouldn't turn his back on a fee.

She tucked the sheet into the couch, frowning as her hand encountered a foreign object in the cushions. She pulled out a petrified licorice stick and threw it into the garbage. The man was a slob and a lowlife. But if he found Sam, she would pay him enough to buy as much licorice as he wanted for the rest of his life.

She turned out the light, plunging the room into darkness, then made her way to the sofa. She stretched out, and her thoughts drifted. For most of her life being a wealthy Baker had been both a blessing and a curse, either drawing people with false motives toward her or allowing her the freedom to follow her own dreams.

If not for her inheritance she wouldn't be able to afford to hire Gideon Graves. And certainly she didn't know whether to consider his presence in her life as a blessing or a curse... although at the moment she definitely leaned toward it being a curse.

Chapter Five

He wasn't sure exactly what pulled him from his sleep. Gideon opened his eyes and stared into the semidarkness of the room. The houseboat rocked softly, occasionally bumping against the dock, the sound familiar and reassuring. Moonlight streamed into the window, and in the distance he heard the splash of a jumping fish. Nothing seemed amiss. So why was he awake?

He sat up and grabbed a pair of jeans, too wide awake to attempt sleep again. Half-dressed, he went to his window and saw Colleen standing on the deck, staring out across the vast expanse of water. *That's what woke me,* he thought, realizing he must have subconsciously heard the opening and closing of the front door when she'd stepped outside.

She looked lonely, a sole figure on a moon-kissed deck. The light breeze off the water stirred her hair, and she wrapped her arms around herself, as if warding off some inner chill. She was obviously deep in thought. What was she thinking? His eyes narrowed as he continued to stare at her. What possible schemes could she be cooking up in that pretty little head of hers?

On impulse, he left his bedroom, walked through the living room and out the front door. The night was unusually warm for the time of year. Gideon breathed deeply of the balmy, salty air.

As he approached Colleen, she whirled around, and her eyes widened. "Oh, Gideon, you scared me." She breathed an audible sigh of relief.

"Can't sleep?" He joined her at the railing. His gaze followed hers out across the water, where the light from the nearly full moon painted silver hues on the surface of the waves.

"My father has been murdered, my brother is on the run. My home was broken into, and somebody might be tapping my phone. I've got more than a few things on my mind." She turned once again and looked at him. "So, what's your excuse?"

He shrugged and leaned forward with his elbows on the railing. "I just woke up and decided to get some fresh air."

"I never got to sleep in the first place." Once again she turned her attention toward the expanse of water. For a long moment neither of them spoke. The only sound was the rhythmic whoosh of the waves as they splashed against the side of the boat.

"It's beautiful here," she said, breaking the relative silence. "So serene, so peaceful. How long have you lived here?"

"For three years."

"Since you resigned from the police force?" He looked at her in surprise, and she smiled. "You aren't the only one capable of doing a little background checking."

He frowned, wondering how deep she had dug into his past, how much she knew about the circumstances surrounding his resignation.

"So what made you decide to quit the police department?" she asked. He relaxed. She apparently hadn't dug too deep. "Wait, let me guess." She faced him, the moonlight illuminating her features in its bewitching glow. "You're a rebel and didn't want to follow the rules. A lone wolf who follows his own brand of justice."

Gideon laughed, wondering if she and Eddy enjoyed the same reading material. "Not quite. Actually, I loved being a cop." His laughter died abruptly. "My personal life got in the way and made it impossible for me to continue."

She looked at him curiously. "Personal life?"

"My wife," he answered flatly. "Although the lady and I are no longer married." He straightened up, not comfortable with the personal turn of the conversation. "What about you? What made you choose the name Jensen?"

"I didn't choose it, I married it." She smiled. "The gentleman and I are no longer married."

"But you chose to keep the name rather than go back to your maiden name?"

She nodded slowly. "I like being Colleen Jensen," she answered simply.

He wasn't sure he understood what she meant, but decided to press no further. Apparently besides both of them being divorced, they also shared a dislike of others prying into their personal lives. "Tell me about your sisters."

"Carolyn is the oldest of the girls. She lives in Casey's Corners, Kansas. She's happily married to the sheriff there." Her voice was soft, her affection for her siblings obvious. She grinned. "And then there's Bonnie. She's fun, kind of wild and free. She went to Casey's Corners to visit Carolyn and ended up marrying the deputy there a few weeks ago. They're both settled, happy and raising families."

"Are you close to them?"

"Yes, but it's been more difficult with them being so far away. Besides, I wasn't as close to them as I was to Sam."

"Now tell me about Sam," he said, deciding to use this sleepless time to his advantage. She smiled, her features softened by her obvious affection for her brother. Gideon felt a jolt in the pit of his stomach.

Had anyone in his life ever smiled like that at thoughts of him?

Certainly Anne hadn't. At first he'd viewed his wife's smiles as precious gifts rarely given. It wasn't until later he realized they weren't gifts at all, but rather subtle manipulations.

Colleen stepped away from the railing and leaned against the side of the houseboat. Her features were obscured in shadows. "Have you ever had a hero, Gideon?" she asked. He shook his head, and she continued, "Never? Not even when you were young?"

"There were no heroes in my life," he answered, trying to focus on her words rather than the way the breeze pressed her pajama top intimately against her body. The pajamas were tailored, cotton fabric, not in any way revealing, and yet he found them strangely sexy.

"Too bad. Everyone needs a hero. Sam is mine."

"And what makes Sam such a paragon of virtue?" Gideon asked dryly.

She laughed. Low and sexy, her laughter rode the breeze. "Oh, believe me, Sam is no paragon of virtue. He's stubborn as a mule and a workaholic. He's got a hot temper and hates to be told he's wrong about anything."

"Then what makes him hero material?" Gideon asked. So far, she'd described a man much like himself, and God knew, Gideon certainly was no hero.

"Despite all his very human faults, Sam has the most giving spirit I've ever known. He possesses an innate gentleness and a strong, unyielding code of honor...." Her voice trailed off, and her smile fell apart. "I can't believe he's gotten himself into this kind of trouble."

"You don't think he's guilty?"

"Of course not," she answered without hesitation. "He could never, under any circumstances, take another life."

"There's absolutely no doubt in your mind?"

Her eyes glittered as she looked at him. "None," she said firmly.

Gideon found her faith admirable, if perhaps naive. "And what makes you so sure? What facts do you have to support your belief in his innocence?"

She tilted her head and smiled yet again. "No facts, just faith."

He fought against his impulse to snort with derision. "It's been my experience that faith is for fools."

"I'd say we've had very different experiences."

"I'm sure that is an understatement," he replied.

She eyed him curiously, started to speak, then instead directed her gaze toward the bay. He watched her as she stepped forward and leaned toward the railing.

With her features immobile and awash in the pale moonlight, she looked like the figurehead of a ship. The breeze sculpted her hair away from her face and once again molded her pajama top to her curves. The vision was dispelled as her breasts rose and fell on a deep sigh.

"Sam used to say that moonlight was magical, that nobody could tell a lie when standing in the light of the moon." Wistfulness stirred her features. "That's what I miss most. Sam always made me believe such things were really possible."

For a brief moment Gideon wished he, too, had the capacity to make her believe such things were possible. He rubbed his forehead, confused by the warmth of strange emotion she provoked. She was appealing, far too appealing for comfort. Immediately, anger swept through him. "Sounds like a bunch of nonsense to me," he retorted. "I'm going back to bed. One of us better be functioning with some sleep tomorrow." He started to go inside.

"Gideon?"

He paused and turned to her. "What?"

"Did you love her?" she asked softly. "I mean your wife?"

He wanted to lie, denounce those long-ago feelings he'd once experienced. But as he gazed at Colleen, bathed in the silver incandescence, her eyes searching his face so trustingly, he couldn't. "More than life," he whispered. "It was a mistake I'll never make again."

"Getting married?"

"No. Loving." Realizing he'd said more than he intended, exposed a private area of his soul, he twirled on his heels and went inside.

* * *

Colleen looked at her watch for the third time in as many minutes. Gideon should be here any second to pick her up and take her to her duplex. Yawning, she thought longingly of being in her own home, sleeping in her own bed, away from Gideon's disturbing presence.

Those moments in the middle of the night in the moonlight with him had been very disturbing. Clad only in his jeans, his chest bronzed and bare, his physical presence had been enough to put her on edge. More than the power of his very maleness had been the depth of his emotion when he'd told her what little he'd said about his ex-wife.

"More than life." She had heard the betrayal in his voice and ached when she remembered him stating so firmly that he would never love again. Despite hurting for him, she understood completely. She, too, had been disillusioned with love.

Jesse Jensen had made promises, taken vows, but when he realized she didn't want to live the life-style her money afforded her, he walked away in disgust, letting Colleen know it had never been her he loved. Only the money. Always the money.

The day after Jesse left her, she decided if she ever fell in love again, it would be with a man who had his own wealth and didn't need the thought of hers to make her appealing.

Putting her files away, she dismissed these thoughts, realizing overtiredness was making her maudlin. Desk cleaned off, she left her office, deciding to wait for Gideon outside.

The afternoon sunshine was warm on her shoulders as she sank down on the bus stop bench at the curb in front of the social services building. The leaves on the trees had already turned brown, and although the sun was warm, Colleen was aware that winter was just around the corner. Winter, with cold winds and snow.

Would Sam be someplace warm? How was he eating, where was he staying? Colleen knew his bank accounts had been frozen by the police, and Sam had never been one to carry large amounts of cash on him. When he'd run on the night of the murder, Colleen would have guessed he probably had less than fifty dollars in his wallet.

She leaned her head back and closed her eyes, tilting her face toward the sun, surprised when her mental vision of Sam was displaced by an image of Gideon. Odd, how much the private eye reminded her of Sam. The two men seemed to have the same quirky sense of humor, an inner silent strength that was slightly daunting.

A squeal of tires made her snap her eyes open in time to see a car veer toward the curb where she sat. Before she could move, a man jumped out of the passenger side of the car and raced toward her. With one hand he grabbed her purse as the other hand reached for her throat.

Instinctively Colleen fought back, gasping in pain as his fingers raked the tender flesh of her neck. She tumbled off the bench, trying to maintain her hold on her purse and at the same time get away. Her senses swam as the back of her head connected with the concrete sidewalk.

"Hey, you son of a..."

In the distance Colleen heard Gideon's yell, followed by the pounding of running footsteps. Her attacker released her and jumped in the waiting car. With a burning squeal of tires, the car sped away.

Gideon reached her just as she sat up. His face was a mask of fury. "Are you all right?" he asked as he extended a hand to help her stand.

She nodded, too shaken to speak for a moment. Despite the fact that she was now on her feet, she was grateful Gideon didn't release her hand. He seemed to sense her need of the human, physical connection. "At least I didn't let him get my purse," she said shakily.

"What exactly happened?" he asked.

She shrugged. "I was sitting on the bench waiting for you. He jumped out of a car and grabbed at me." She squeezed his hand tightly, then finally released it. "Thank God you showed up when you did."

"You're bleeding," he said. His eyes narrowed as he focused on her neck.

She reached up and touched the tender area beneath the chain of her necklace. "Just scratches," she replied.

He placed an arm around her shoulder, and she gratefully leaned into him. "Come on, let's go to my place, and I'll clean you up." He smiled, his eyes filled with a tenderness that soothed the wounds more effectively than any antiseptic.

Although moments before she had been anticipating the return to her own place, she didn't argue with the idea of going to Gideon's instead.

"I've got more bad news," Gideon said once they were in his car and heading toward the houseboat. She stifled a groan and looked at him expectantly. "My friend swept your duplex. He found several bugs and a tap on your telephone line."

She stared at him. "The police?" she finally asked.

He shook his head. "We don't think so. The equipment was very high-tech, far more expensive than what the police department uses."

"Then who?" Colleen whispered, a shiver racing through her.

"That's what we need to find out."

She leaned her head against the seat, wincing as she realized the back of her skull was sore. She rubbed the area, unsurprised to find a lump the size of a walnut. "I feel like I'm playing a game where somebody neglected to tell me the rules." She looked at Gideon once again. "Only this isn't a game, is it?"

He smiled. "If it is, I think it's one we shouldn't play."

She frowned and rubbed her head once again. "I can't believe, on top of everything else, I got mugged."

Gideon turned into the marina parking lot and found a space. He shut off the car, then turned and looked at her. "Colleen, I don't think it was a case of a random mugging attempt. Following on the heels of your apartment being searched yesterday, it's just too much of a coincidence."

"You don't believe in coincidences?"

"Not this kind."

Together they got out of the car and walked down the ramp toward his boat. The evening sun was kind to the structure, softening the stark reality of peeling paint and disrepair.

"Why don't you sit there," he said, gesturing toward a chair at the kitchen table once they were inside. As she sank down at the table he disappeared into the bathroom, returning a moment later with a first-aid kit. "Colleen," he began as he sat on the chair next to her and opened the tin container. "I think you should stay here for a couple of days, until we get a handle on what's going on."

She frowned thoughtfully. She hated this, the feeling of her life out of her control. She also wasn't sure she wanted to stay in these close quarters with Gideon. However, the thought of being all alone in an impersonal hotel room was even less appealing. "Okay," she finally agreed.

"I also don't think you should go to work for the next couple of days," he added.

"Oh, I can't do that," she protested. "People depend on me to be there."

"And whoever came after you today knew you'd be there, too," he reminded her.

Her frown deepened. He was right. "I'll have to call Margie and see if she can cover my cases for a couple of days." She looked at him. "Do you think we'll have some answers in that time?"

"I don't know," he admitted. "But it seems to me that suddenly the stakes have gotten higher. If the break-in yesterday and the attack this afternoon are any indication, somebody is getting desperate for something, and I imagine it's just a matter of time before they show their hand."

He took a cotton ball and soaked it with hydrogen peroxide. "Now, sit back and let Dr. Gideon take care of your neck."

She nodded and leaned her head back, exposing the bloody scratch marks to his view. His stomach clenched with anger as he saw her soft skin so viciously marred. He stood up, bending over her, and gently moved the material of her blouse aside. She winced as he applied the medicated cotton ball to the scratches. "What in the hell was he trying to do to you?" he muttered as he cleaned off the blood.

"He went for my purse first, then started clawing at my neck. I thought...I thought he was trying to kill me," she answered softly.

Again anger swept through him. His insides twisted and his hand shook slightly as he worked silently. If only he'd arrived to pick her up a few minutes earlier.

If only he'd been able to get the license plate number of the car.

As he cleaned out the scratches, he was aware of the sweet, scented perfume that emanated from her. He tried to focus only on the wounds, but found himself distracted by the tiny pulse that throbbed in the hollow of her throat. He was far too conscious of her body heat warming him as he leaned over her, the way the gold of her necklace seemed dull in comparison to the lustrous hue of her skin.

The scratches were clean, but still he lingered, rubbing a fresh cotton ball gently over a greater expanse of her neck, half mesmerized by the creaminess of her skin, the satiny texture that seemed to beg to be touched.

She closed her eyes, as if finding pleasure in his physical contact, and a flame of desire swept through him, desire so intense it shocked him. He wanted to kiss her, wanted to taste her lips. He knew instinctively they would be as sweet as the scent of her perfume. He wanted to press his lips against the pulse at the base of her throat, run his hands over the curve of her breasts.

He threw the cotton ball onto the table as if it were on fire. "That should do it," he said gruffly as he stepped away from her.

She opened her eyes. "Thank you," she murmured.

"No problem," he replied. "I wouldn't want you to get tetanus and die before I collect my fee from you."

She flushed. "We certainly wouldn't want that."

He flashed her a hard smile. "Man does not live on bread alone. Speaking of bread, how about dinner?" He got up and reached into a drawer and pulled out half a dozen carry-out menus. "Let's see, we've got pizza, Chinese, a chicken place. What's your pleasure?"

"Do you have all your meals delivered?" Colleen asked.

"Of course not. I usually go out for breakfast and lunch. I rarely cook."

"Don't you get tired of eating out? Why don't I just whip something up for dinner?" She stood up and went to the refrigerator. Peering inside, she saw he had eggs, milk, a chunk of Cheddar cheese. "I could make omelets," she offered. She closed the door, realizing she was being presumptuous. "Unless you don't want me messing up your kitchen."

"No, please help yourself. I just assumed you didn't cook."

"I'm not a gourmet, but I enjoy puttering around in the kitchen." In truth, Colleen needed the physical activity to keep her thoughts of Gideon at bay.

As she busied herself finding a skillet and getting the makings for the omelets out of the refrigerator, she was intensely aware of Gideon's gaze on her.

He sat in a chair at the table, his eyes following her every movement as his fingers drummed absently on the top of the table. "I think I'll get some fresh air," he finally said.

Colleen breathed a sigh of relief as he got up and disappeared out the door. She hadn't realized how tense she had been until he left and seemed to take much of the tension with him.

And she knew where much of that tension had come from. It had begun the moment he touched her. When he'd leaned over her, enveloping her in his masculine scent, a knot of yearning had formed in the pit of her stomach.

As she whipped the eggs in a bowl and melted butter in the skillet, she remembered the feel of him touching her throat. His hands had been hot, almost fevered. There had been a moment when his ministrations had changed from the detached care of a stranger to the languid caress of a lover. Her pulse quickened at the memory as she contemplated what kind of a lover Gideon would be.

Passionate. Intense. She had a feeling he would be both. He would be single-minded and demand the same sort of intensity from his partner.

Oh, how she longed to feel passion again. Her work had been the only thing in her life to inspire that particular emotion in the last couple of years.

She knew already that Gideon was a man capable of deep emotions, knew it from the way he had told her he'd loved his wife more than life itself. She wondered what had happened between Gideon and his wife. Where had the love gone? Had it simply died, or had it never really existed except in his own mind, as it had happened with her and Jesse?

Colleen realized the love she'd thought she'd seen in Jesse's eyes had been nothing more than hidden calculation and greed. She'd fooled herself, wanting to believe his love was real, ignoring all the little signals that should have told her differently.

She frowned as she poured the egg mixture into the awaiting skillet. She couldn't forget why she was here. She couldn't allow herself to feel anything for Gideon Graves expect gratitude that he was allowing her to stay here until they decided she was out of danger. He wanted nothing more from her than his fee.

Getting involved with Gideon on any other basis than strictly business would be pure foolish. Gideon, like Jesse, was interested in the monetary benefit of a relationship with her. Although, unlike Jesse, Gideon was honest and open in the fact that he wanted her money in return for his services in seeking Sam. She was far too smart to make the same mistake twice in a lifetime. She would never again allow a man to fool her into believing he loved her when all he really wanted was the pleasure of her money.

She was here because Gideon thought she would be safe here from whatever madness was going on in her life. He would protect her from anyone trying to harm her. Still, as she remembered the heat of his touch, the fire of desire he'd ignited inside her, she wondered who was going to protect her from herself....

Chapter Six

Gideon stood on the deck, watching as the evening shadows usurped the sunlight. It was odd, to stand on the deck and listen to the sounds of somebody else bustling in his kitchen. Since the time he had moved in three years ago, no woman had been in the houseboat until now. Until Colleen.

The rattle of dishes drifted out the window, along with the sound of her humming as she worked. He could smell the scent of eggs cooking and coffee perking. He leaned against the railing and thought about the woman inside his residence.

The circumstances surrounding the bugging of her duplex and the attack on her that afternoon were just a few of the things that confused him about her.

Far more confusing than the circumstances that had brought her here in the first place was his response to her and her presence in his house, in his life.

For the first time in what seemed like forever he was thinking of things other than work, other than the mere routine of survival. Instead, as he watched the sun slowly dip down beyond the horizon, he found himself thinking of things he hadn't thought of in years.

Things like the pleasure of feminine companionship. Sharing coffee in the quiet beauty of dawn, small talk that meant nothing and yet connected the souls. Quiet moments when conversation wasn't necessary to communicate, when words were transmitted through a glance, a touch. And finally he thought about the heady rush of sexual tension.

He swiped a hand through his hair, grateful for the cool breeze that he hoped would banish the heat still rolling around inside him. He shouldn't have touched her. That had been his initial mistake. He should have let her clean her neck by herself. He should have thrown her the cotton balls and the peroxide and left her to her own devices.

He frowned as he thought again of the circumstances that had forced her here. There was no doubt in his mind that the tossing of her home and the mugging were related. Somebody wanted something from her, but what? He believed her when she maintained she didn't know. He'd seen the confusion muddy her eyes, the fear of the unknown.

Besides, there was no way on earth she would be here with him if those events hadn't frightened her immensely.

She was out of his league. She was a Baker, cut of the same social ilks as Anne. It didn't matter that her skin was soft and tempting. It wasn't important that the scent of her stirred his senses. He wasn't looking to get involved with any woman. He preferred his aloneness, where he wasn't vulnerable.

"Gideon?"

He jumped at the sound of her voice and turned to look at her. "Yes?"

"The omelets are ready."

He nodded and followed her inside, surprised to see she had set the table, complete with colorful place mats he'd forgotten he owned. For some reason the sight of the gaily striped place mats irritated him, adding a touch of feminine domesticity where there had been none. "I'm surprised you can cook," he said as he sat down at the table. "I would have assumed as a member of the Baker dynasty you had somebody to do those sort of mundane things for you."

She sliced the omelet in two and slid half onto his plate and the other half onto her own. "When I was growing up we had a cook, but I decided a long time ago that I wasn't going to live the life-style of my youth." She grabbed a saucer containing a tower of toast slices, added it to the table, then sat down in the chair across from him. "Besides, unlike you, I don't like to eat out or have food delivered very often."

He gazed at her in disbelief. "I've never met a woman who didn't like to eat out as frequently as possible."

"You've met one now," she answered, then smiled at his continued skepticism. "Believe what you want, Gideon. I have a strong self-identity. I don't need your beliefs about me to confirm who I am."

Again an unwanted admiration swept through him as he heard the confidence that rang in her voice. "I suppose it's easier to find yourself when you have plenty of money to decide who you are," he observed.

She paused, a piece of toast in her hand, her gaze thoughtful as she looked at him. "Do you only hate women who have money, or do you hate women in general?"

He looked at her in surprise. "I certainly don't hate women." He frowned, wondering how to explain to her his disdain, his mistrust of the very wealthy. "It's just been my experience that people who have a lot of money rarely have any ethics to go with it."

"My father was a very ethical man. I didn't always agree with his choice of priorities, but I never doubted that he had great character and integrity." She paused a moment, cutting her omelet into dainty little bites. "What about your parents...what were they like?"

"My father left when I was ten, and my mother worked herself to death as a waitress to provide the essentials." He was pleased that his words held no emotion, simply a statement of bald facts.

"Did you ever see your father again?" she asked, her voice gentle.

"As a matter of fact, I did. He showed up at my graduation ceremony from the police academy." Immediately he could remember the shock, the utter surprise that had filled him when he'd seen the man who was his father sitting in the audience. Gideon leaned back in his chair, reflecting for a moment. "When the ceremony was over he came up to me, hugged me and told me how proud he was. As a child, I'd dreamed of hearing words like that from him, but when he finally spoke them they didn't mean anything. I realized my father was nothing more than a stranger to me."

Colleen reached up and touched the charm that hung on the gold chain around her neck, her face radiating sadness. "I know how difficult that is. I felt the same way when my father died. I was upset but suddenly realized he'd never been a very big part of my life. I always assumed we'd have time in the future... to become closer, develop a bond. It was the hardest moment of my life, when I had to face the knowledge that there were no more chances for us to be close."

Gideon felt a strange connection with her, the knowledge that despite their diverse backgrounds they had both lacked the gift of a strong paternal presence in their lives. The fact that they had anything at all in common only increased his general discomfort. He grabbed a piece of toast and tore it in half. "We'd better eat before it gets cold," he said abruptly, effectively stifling any further conversation she might want to make.

When they finished eating, they cleared the table. "If we'd ordered out we could have just thrown the paper plates away," he said as she filled the sink with soapy water and he carried the last dish from the table to the countertop.

"This will only take a minute," she replied smoothly, then smiled as she handed him a dish towel. "Besides, haven't you heard? Washing and drying dishes builds character."

"I didn't realize I was lacking in that particular department," he protested.

She grinned. "The jury is still out on that subject." She handed him a clean, dripping plate.

"So what made you become a social worker?" Gideon asked as he dried the plate, then placed it in the appropriate cabinet.

She shrugged. "I can't remember a time when I didn't want to do something to help people. Social work seemed like the logical choice. I decided to work with family services because I wanted to be an advocate for children's rights."

"Lofty ambitions," he observed, taking the glass she held out.

"Perhaps, but I felt it was important to give back some of the good life has given me. And that reminds me, as soon as we finish here, I really need to call Margie and make sure she can cover for me for a few days. She'll probably agree, but she won't be happy about it."

Gideon nodded absently, again confused by her. He wanted to believe she was frivolous, a wealthy young woman playing the role of social worker for fun. But when she spoke of her work, it was obvious it was important to her, obvious she was committed. Anne had never been committed to anything except herself and shopping.

They finished the last of the dishes in a companionable silence. "While you're calling Margie, I'm going to get the bedroom ready for you. I insist," he said as she started to protest.

As she picked up the phone, he went into the bedroom and started stripping the sheets off the bed. He tried not to think of his task, preparing her bed for the night, afraid he'd reawaken the flare of desire that had swept through him as he'd cleaned her wounds. It was far too easy to imagine her in the bed, her hair a rich, dark cloud against the pale sheets, her smoky blue eyes hazy with sleep . . . or desire. He shook his head to banish the image.

It was probably a mistake having her here under his roof. She was definitely a physical temptation. And she was also in some sort of danger. It was a compelling combination. He grinned, thinking of what Eddy would say. "A gorgeous dame with sexy legs, a hardboiled P.I. with a chip on his shoulder. Trouble with a capital T."

Pulling out a clean set of sheets from one of the drawers, he frowned, wondering why Eddy hadn't been around all day. It was unusual for the kid not to make a daily appearance. He hoped everything was all right. Gideon had enough trouble on his hands trying to figure out how to help the shapely package of dynamite sitting in his kitchen.

"Can I help?" Colleen asked, standing hesitantly in the doorway of the bedroom.

"Sure, you can get on the other side of the bed." As she moved into position, he threw half the fitted sheet to her. They worked together, putting on the bottom sheet then adding the flat one.

"You know this really isn't necessary," she said as they finished up. "I could have slept on the sofa."

"I'm more comfortable with you being in here. This way you'll have your privacy for all the rituals women do before they go to bed and when they get up in the morning."

She grinned, her eyes sparkling with amusement. "Rituals?"

To his horror, Gideon felt a blush warm his face. "You know, all the powdering and lotioning and skin-cream stuff that women do."

She laughed, the sound filled with the music of mirth. Despite his embarrassment Gideon felt a reluctant grin stretching his lips. His grin seemed to feed her laughter, and she collapsed onto the bed, gales of merriment causing tears to sparkle in her eyes.

Someplace in the back of his mind, he knew her laughter was a product of her tension, a natural release of the fear and anxiety that had been inside her since the moment they had walked into her ransacked duplex. He could hear the slight edge of hysteria in her laugh, knew she had momentarily lost control.

He didn't care what caused it, didn't even care if she was in some way laughing at him. He simply wanted to enjoy her laughter. With a pang he realized his life had been void of that particular expression for too long.

She sat up, swiping her tears with the back of one hand. "I'm sorry... I'm not even sure why I'm laughing," she finally managed to gasp. "It's just that I'm lucky if I get the time to use soap and water on my face. I don't even own a jar of skin cream." She giggled helplessly and fell back on the bed.

He couldn't help but notice how dark and rich her hair appeared next to the paleness of the sheets. He was aware of her perfume, that damned pleasant scent that made him think of fields of flowers and making love.

Although he tried, he couldn't ignore the heat that began as an ember in the pit of his stomach and grew into an inferno as it spread to his extremities.

Barely aware of his actions, he held out a hand to help her up. As she slipped her hand in his, he pulled her off the bed. Her laughter died the moment her feet touched the floor. She stood so close to him he felt the heat emanating from her, felt the warmth of her breath on his throat.

The lips that had moments before been laughing, now tempted him beyond reason. He wanted to taste their sweetness, wanted them to open to him in eagerness. Her eyes widened and she gasped softly, as if she saw his desire, felt it herself. The blue of her eyes darkened, and she raised her chin, a subtle offering of her lips to him.

With a deep moan, he lowered his head and touched his mouth to hers.

"Hey Gideon. Are you home?"

At the sound of Eddy's voice they jumped apart, like guilty teenagers caught by a vigilant parent. Colleen cleared her throat, her gaze not quite meeting his. "Who's that?"

Gideon sighed and ripped a hand through his hair. "Come on out and meet my partner."

"Your partner?" she said with surprise. "I...I didn't know you had one."

As Eddy called out again, Gideon grimaced. "Fast Eddy. He's got a lot of enthusiasm, but his timing isn't so great," he said dryly.

She looked at him again, this time her eyes holding the boldness he'd come to expect from her. "I'd say his timing is perfect."

He returned her gaze for a long moment, then nodded, a silent assent. Yes, he was sure she was right. Eddy's timing had been perfect, keeping them from making a crazy, impulsive mistake. And Gideon was certain kissing Colleen was a mistake.

In the brief moment that their lips had touched, he'd realized a single kiss would not be enough to sate him. Better to stop before starting, and Gideon had a feeling if Eddy hadn't walked in when he had, there would have been no stopping.

Colleen awoke to the sun shining through the small porthole above the bed. She jolted upright, for a moment thinking she must be late for work. Then she remembered. She was at Gideon's houseboat and she wasn't going to work today.

She nestled beneath the sheet and closed her eyes, allowing the languid heaviness of sleep to overtake her again. At the same time her mind replayed the events of the night before.

They had stayed up until long after midnight, Eddy, Gideon and herself, talking about Sam and the murder, throwing out theories with no basis, suppositions that led nowhere.

She smiled as she thought of the red-haired teenager. It had been obvious he worshiped Gideon and equally obvious that Eddy's attentions exasperated Gideon. However, beneath his exasperation, Colleen had sensed Gideon's genuine, if reluctant, affection for the kid.

They were an odd couple, Eddy appearing to be so needy and Gideon seeming to need nothing and no one. Stirring restlessly, she thought of that moment just before Eddy had arrived, that single instant when Gideon's lips had touched hers.

His mouth had been hot and had tasted of need, the raw need of a man for a woman. He seemed to have no need for an emotional tie of any kind, but in that instant of her standing so close to him, his body had betrayed a very different kind of need.

She frowned, realizing that the very bed where she lay smelled like Gideon. It was the wonderful, mysterious scent of maleness, and it beckoned to a responding warmth inside her.

Disturbed by her thoughts, she shoved back the sheet and got up. She had barely noticed the room last night when she'd finally gone to bed, and now she looked around with interest.

The room was stark in decor, containing only a full-size bed, a dresser and a desk in one corner with an expensive-looking computer setup. Nothing personal, not even a picture on the wall to give a clue to the personality of the man who lived here.

She walked over to the window, where a cool, salt-kissed breeze drifted in. In the distance, gulls made lazy circles in the sky, occasionally dipping down to scoop up a fish for breakfast.

Breakfast. She turned from the window, anxious for a cup of coffee to chase away any lingering sleepiness. And she needed a shower, a cold one, to banish any residual heat thoughts of Gideon's kiss evoked. She walked to the closed bedroom door and leaned an ear against the wood. Nothing. No sounds from the living room. Gideon had said last night that he intended to leave early this morning to do a little sleuthing. He must already be gone. She grabbed clean clothes for the day, then scampered into the bathroom. Minutes later, showered and dressed, she checked the kitchen cabinets, seeking the coffee.

"Aha," she finally muttered triumphantly, finding a can in the refrigerator. She scooped the appropriate amount for a full pot into the machine, then wandered around the living room as she waited for it to brew.

With a little money and a lot of attention, the houseboat could actually be quite pleasant, she thought. It was roomy yet efficient, and the constant, almost imperceptible rocking movement was soothing.

By looking around it was easy to see that Gideon used it merely as a place to call home, but didn't consider it a home at all. There was nothing personal in the decor, nothing to indicate the kind of man who lived here. Unless she considered the packages of red licorice lying around and a stack of overdue bills that set on one of the end tables.

So what kind of a man was Gideon Graves? He gave off such mixed signals. He made no bones about the fact he abhorred people with money, and yet also made it clear that money was the only reason he'd taken her case. Was it her money that had made him want to kiss her? She frowned. It had certainly worked like an aphrodisiac on Jesse.

She'd just poured her coffee and sat down at the table when a knock sounded at the door. A rush of adrenaline pumped through her as she remembered the events that had brought her here. If somebody had been bugging her duplex, it was quite possible they knew she was here.

"Who's there?" she called out cautiously.

"It's me."

She relaxed at the sound of Eddy's squeaky voice and opened the door. "Hi, Eddy, come on in."

He nodded shyly and stepped inside. "I remembered that last night Gideon said he was going to leave early this morning, and I just thought I'd come by and sort of keep an eye on things here."

Colleen tried to hide a smile as she realized the skinny, awkward teen had come to protect her from any harm. "I appreciate your concern, Eddy," she said, smiling as the tips of his ears turned red with a blush of pleasure. "I was just about to have a cup of coffee. Would you like one?"

"That sounds great," he agreed, then strutted over to the table and sat down.

Colleen poured them each a cup, watching in amusement as he added four spoons of sugar to his before taking a sip and smacking his lips in satisfaction. "You make good coffee, better than Gideon," he said.

She smiled again, wondering how many spoons of sugar Gideon's coffee required. "Have you known Gideon a long time?" she asked.

He shrugged. "A couple of years, but we've gotten pretty close in the last couple of months." Eddy reared back in the chair, as Colleen had seen Gideon do whenever he sat at the table. "Since I graduated from high school last May, I've had a lot more time to spend around here, you know, helping Gideon out."

"You graduated? Good for you. Are you going to college?"

He shook his head. "No money for that. Besides, I'm going to be a private eye like Gideon." His face creased with a huge smile. "Some day everyone who needs an investigator will know that Fast Eddy is one of the best."

"Gideon referred to you as Fast Eddy last night. Where did you get the nickname?"

"I was on the high school track team, broke a couple of running records, so everyone started calling me Fast Eddy," he explained. "I think it's a good name for a P.I., don't you?"

"It's certainly catchy," she agreed.

"Yeah, I'm hoping Gideon will teach me all the tricks to the trade. He's great, isn't he?" Eddy's smile wavered slightly. "Sometimes in my head, I pretend like he's my dad," he blurted, then blushed furiously. He stood up and drained his coffee cup. "Well, I really didn't intend to come in and bother you. I just wanted to tell you I'll be outside keeping an eye on the perimeters, and you shouldn't worry about anything."

"You're welcome to hang around in here, Eddy," she offered as she walked him to the door.

"Thanks, but I think it would be better if I stayed outside. Besides, I brought my fishing pole and tackle, sort of as a disguise. I'll just sit on the bank out there and keep a lookout." He smiled shyly, then with a small wave, he disappeared.

Colleen picked up her coffee cup from the table and carried it with her to the window. She watched as Eddy took a position along the shoreline where he could keep on eye on the houseboat and another on his fishing pole. Sipping her coffee, she wondered about Eddy's family. What kind of a home life did he have? Apparently not great, if he spent much of his time here with Gideon indulging in fantasies of being a famous investigator.

Even more curious was Eddy pretending Gideon was his father. She wondered where Eddy's real father was, if he was a presence in the boy's life. As a social worker, she saw far too many children who didn't have the healthy luxury of both parents in their lives. Colleen herself had been just a toddler when her own mother had died. With her often absent, workaholic father, it wasn't a surprise that she felt particularly close to her siblings.

Thinking of her sisters, Colleen realized she needed to call them and tell them she would be staying here for the next couple of days.

She moved away from the window and filled her coffee cup. Then she sank down onto the sofa and reached for the telephone on the end table.

Punching in Carolyn's number in Casey's Corners, Kansas, she settled against the cushions and realized she was homesick to hear Carolyn's voice. It had been several weeks since the two had spoken. The last time had been the day before their sister Bonnie's wedding. Bonnie had given them little notice of the wedding, and Colleen had been disappointed when a difficult case had prevented her attendance.

"Hello?"

Colleen's heart expanded with warmth at the sound of Carolyn's voice. She hadn't realized how much she had missed her sister since Carolyn had moved away. "Caro, it's me."

"Oh, Colleen, it's so good to hear your voice. I was just thinking about you. How are you? Is everything all right?"

Colleen hesitated a moment, unsure how much to tell her about the events of the last couple of days. "Things are okay," she hedged, deciding not to mention anything. "I just wanted to tell you that I'm not going to be at home for the next couple of days. I'm staying with a—a friend and wanted to give you the number here."

"Hang on, let me get a piece of paper and a pencil." There was a pause. "Okay, I'm ready."

Colleen gave her Gideon's number. "How's Bonnie and her new husband, Russ? I assume the wedding went off without a hitch?"

"It was wonderful. The whole town turned out for the event. Gosh, Colleen, you don't know how much we all wished you could have been here. You . . . and Sam." Carolyn paused a moment and cleared her throat. "Anyway, it was a beautiful ceremony and Bonnie looked radiant. We'd all been so tense since the break-in, it was terrific to have something to celebrate."

"Break-in?" Colleen frowned.

"Yes, somebody broke into the house one night a couple of weeks before the wedding. It was really odd. The only things we found missing were the necklaces that Daddy gave us. Both Bonnie's and mine were stolen."

Colleen's heart seemed to stop beating for a moment. She reached up to her neck, her fingertips cold as she traced the raised welts and scratches. Was it possible? Her mind rebelled at the very thought. Surely it was merely a coincidence?

"Colleen?"

"Yeah, I'm here." She frowned and released her tight hold on the necklace. "Caro, I've got to go. I'll call you later in the week. In the meantime, you've got this number in case you need to reach me."

"Colleen, are you sure everything is all right?"

Colleen could hear the worry in her sister's voice. "I promise. Everything is under control. I love you, Caro, and give Bonnie my love."

"We love you, too," Carolyn replied.

Colleen hung up the phone slowly, her thoughts on the gold charm hanging around her neck. She unclasped the necklace and allowed it to fall into her hand.

Staring at it, she remembered the day her father had given it to her. It had been one of the very rare occasions when her father had called her and asked her to meet him for lunch. They'd dined in a restaurant near the Baker Enterprises headquarters.

Throughout the meal, Joseph Baker had been distant, distracted, but Colleen hadn't thought it unusual. Joseph was usually distracted most of the time. He'd eaten quickly, then pulled out the jeweler's box and handed it to her.

"A gift," he'd said. "I bought one for each of my children." He'd looked at her from across the table, his blue eyes so intense, filled with a love Colleen had never seen before.

She looked at the necklace in her hand, noting the beautiful workmanship of the charm. The mythical phoenix, a symbol of rebirth and immortality. Joseph had been such a pragmatic man. The phoenix had seemed an odd choice to Colleen.

Now, looking back on that day, Colleen wondered if her father had somehow felt a sense of impending doom. Had he bought the necklaces with the knowledge that his own death was near?

Why would anyone want our necklaces? she wondered. Although probably fairly expensive, their monetary value certainly wouldn't warrant somebody traveling to Kansas to steal Bonnie's and Carolyn's, then back to Long Island to obtain Colleen's. It just didn't make any sense. None of it made sense at all.

As she stared at the piece of jewelry, the grief she hadn't felt over the loss of her father suddenly welled up in the back of her throat. For so long following the murder, the grief had been lost amid the horror of the crime itself and Sam's subsequent disappearance.

Tears blurred her vision as she continued to stare at the shiny gold of the mythical bird. Joseph had given her the necklace, kissed her on the forehead, then three days later he'd been killed.

There would be no more chances to get close to her father. With a sob, she put her head down on the table and let her grief consume her.

Chapter Seven

Gideon got out of his car in the marina parking lot and stretched, his arms over his head. Despite the fact that he'd been up for hours, his body was still stiff from sleeping on the sofa. But the kinks in his body were nothing compared to the kinks in his brain.

He'd used every contact he had, every means both legal and illegal he had at his disposal to find Sam Baker. Nothing. It was as if the man had disappeared off the face of the earth. Gideon had never heard of a fugitive who didn't eventually make a mistake, leave an inadvertent clue that led to capture. So how had Sam Baker managed to disappear so completely?

As he walked down the dock toward his houseboat, he realized that if something didn't break soon, he was going to have to tell Colleen he couldn't help her, that he'd failed.

He frowned as he saw Eddy sitting on the shoreline in a fisherman's cap, a pole dangling in the water. Eddy spotted him and grinned widely. He quickly set down the pole and scrambled up the shore toward Gideon.

"Hi, partner," he said cheerfully. "I knew you were going to be gone for awhile this morning so I thought I'd come over and watch over things. You know, keep an eye on the dame."

"Good thinking." He clapped Eddy on the shoulder. "Why don't you continue keeping an eye on things out here, and if you happen to catch enough fish, I'll fry them up for dinner."

"Great!" With a thumbs-up signal, Eddy turned and ran to his pole.

Ah, to be that young and so easily contented, Gideon thought as he walked to the houseboat. Perhaps that was part of Eddy's appeal. Despite the knocks life had given him, the kid had managed to maintain an innocence, an exuberance that Gideon envied. His own innocence had been stolen early in his life, and whatever exuberance he'd once had, whatever visions he'd once entertained for his future had been taken by Anne.

All thoughts of Eddy fell away as he walked into the houseboat and heard Colleen's sobs. She sat on the sofa, her face hidden in her hands, and the sound of her crying touched a place in Gideon's heart that hadn't been touched in a very long time.

It was obvious she was unaware of his entrance, and for a moment he stood by the door awkwardly, unsure what to do. When she continued her mournful sobs, he approached her. "Colleen?" He called her name softly, hesitantly. "What's wrong?"

She looked up in surprise, her face tear-streaked and sorrowful. She stood and quickly swiped at her tears.

"I'm sorry...it's really silly." She attempted a smile, but it crumbled and tears began again. Holding out her arms, she stumbled toward him. "It just hit me...my dad is gone. He's gone forever."

Gideon met her halfway across the room and wrapped his arms around her, holding her tight as she buried her face in his shirtfront and cried.

He didn't know what had prompted her grief, but it didn't much matter. It was odd. He'd believed himself to be inured to feminine tears. During his marriage to Anne, he'd quickly learned that like her smiles, tears could manipulate. It hadn't taken him long to remain unmoved by Anne's false tears.

But he knew Colleen's tears were real, and her pain touched him, made him ache for her. He ran a hand through her hair in an attempt to soothe. "It's all right," he whispered. "Let it all out."

He could smell the scent of his minty soap as well as the fresh, familiar smell of his shampoo. It seemed so intimate, the fact that she'd stood in his shower and used his things.

Holding Colleen was a pleasure, despite her tears. Her body leaned into his, soft and yielding. She held him tight, as if he was her strength, her anchor, and again he felt a curious swirling of emotions deep within. His emotions had little to do with passion or desire. What he felt was more gentle and much more frightening.

"I'm so sorry." She finally pulled away from him, her gaze not meeting his. "I feel so ridiculous. I just started thinking about my dad, and suddenly I was crying and couldn't stop." She tried a smile. "How was your morning?"

"A little less intense than yours." He led her to the table, where she sat down, then he poured them each a cup of coffee. "You sure you're all right?"

She nodded and smiled sheepishly. "To be perfectly honest, I feel better. I guess that cry had been bottled up inside for too long." A blush swept over her face. "I'm sorry. I don't often cry."

He believed her. He couldn't imagine Colleen being the type of woman to use tears to exploit or control. "I saw the resident watchdog outside," he said as he joined her at the table.

"You mean Eddy? Yes, he stopped in and had a cup of coffee with me." She smiled indulgently. "He's something else. He told me he knew you'd be gone this morning so he wanted to guard the perimeters."

Gideon laughed and shook his head. "And he told me he was keeping an eye on the dame."

"He called me a dame?"

"He reads too many Mickey Spillane novels."

"Then I suppose I can forgive him," she said with a small laugh. "Where is his family? He seems to be rather alone."

"For all intents and purposes, he is. His house is about a mile down the beach." He leaned back and propped his chair against the wall, the front legs off the ground. "His father is a truck driver, on the road most of the time. His mother is an alcoholic. If she's home, she's passed out."

"Eddy seems like a bright boy. It's a shame he's not going on to college or any kind of a trade school."

Gideon eyed her with a touch of humor. "Do I see the spinning of a social worker's mind?"

She shrugged and smiled again. "I'd at least like to talk to him about options." She eyed him slyly. "Or you could. He seems to hang on your every word. You could be an important role model for him."

Gideon frowned, uncomfortable with the turn of the conversation. His chair came down hard on the floor. "You don't know anything about me. I'm the last person to be anyone's role model. My life has already been pretty screwed up. Why would I want to take the responsibility for somebody else's life?" He didn't realize how angry he sounded until he saw her flinch. He raked a hand through his hair and drew in a deep breath. "Look, I'm sorry. But you're the social worker, not me. I'm the last person who should try to help anyone decide what's best for them."

She nodded, her gaze not quite as warm on him as it had been moments before. For some reason Gideon felt as if he'd lost something. It irritated him. Suddenly she irritated him. He downed his coffee and stood up. "I spent the morning speaking with a friend of mine, a police officer. There have been hundreds of leads on Sam, but none of them led anywhere. I've got to tell you, Colleen, I'm not sure I can help you on this."

She jumped up suddenly. "I forgot to tell you, I think I have a clue to everything that has happened." She walked over to the coffee table, picked something up, then approached him. She opened up her hand and showed him what she held.

"Your necklace? What does that have to do with anything?" he asked.

"I'm not sure."

He listened as she explained about her conversation with her sister. When she told him about the two stolen necklaces, Gideon felt a quickening of his pulse. He lifted the charm from the palm of her hand, his gaze on the scratches still vivid on her neck. Had this been the object the mugger had been after? Had the grab for her purse merely been a diversion?

He looked at the necklace, a pretty piece, obviously expensive, but he couldn't imagine how it could possibly be a part of any of this. Still... he flipped it over, squinting as he spied tiny writing across the bottom. "What is this?" he asked.

Colleen looked at it in surprise. "I don't know. I never noticed it before."

"I suppose it could be the artist's signature," he said thoughtfully.

"Do you think this is all-important, or do you think it's just coincidence that both Carolyn's and Bonnie's necklaces were stolen?"

He frowned, his gaze once again going to the scratches around her neck. "This is one of those coincidences that just doesn't feel right." Once again he stared at the tiny writing across the bottom of the charm. He shook his head in frustration. "I can't read it. It's just too small."

"Do you own a magnifying glass?" she asked.

He shook his head. "You know where your father bought these?"

"I imagine he bought them all at Lowensteins in Manhattan. That's where Dad always bought jewelry."

"Then perhaps we should take a drive into Manhattan. If we're lucky we'll be able to find some answers there."

"Should we invite Eddy to take the ride with us?" she asked.

He looked at her sharply. "No. If you want to redeem Eddy, do it on your own time. Let's go." Without waiting for her, he went out the door. He knew he'd been brusque. Hell, he'd been nothing short of a bastard. But he had the distinct feeling Little Miss Social Worker wouldn't be satisfied just offering help to Eddy. She would somehow get it into her head to redeem Gideon. She would never understand that he was a fallen angel. He was simply not redeemable.

The drive to Lowensteins on Broadway would take just a little over an hour. The first half hour of the drive was accomplished in silence.

Colleen couldn't help it. His brusqueness before they left had hurt her feelings. Twice in the conversation he'd snapped at her, both times taking her by surprise.

She found it interesting that each time he'd become short the conversation had involved Eddy and role models. She turned in the passenger seat and cast him a surreptitious gaze.

On the morning she'd first met him, she'd thought he looked wild and half-crazy, with his intense eyes and unruly hair. She realized she now found his unmanageable hair sexy and his dark gaze intriguing. It held secrets she wanted to learn, experiences she wanted to share.

Frowning, she turned to stare out the window, wondering what secrets of his past made him so afraid to reach out to anyone else. She had no doubt it was fear that had inspired his anger. He'd said his life was screwed up, and he didn't want the responsibility of being Eddy's role model. Her disappointment in him had taken her by surprise.

She rubbed two fingers across her forehead where a dull ache had begun. With everything that was going on in her life, why on earth was she wasting time trying to figure out a licorice-chewing, recalcitrant man who was only in her life because she was paying for his time?

Leaning her head against the seat, she released a deep sigh. She just wanted this over with. She wanted the real murderer of her father found. She wanted Sam home where he belonged, and she wanted to go back to the uncomplicated life she'd led before her father's death.

"You're awfully quiet," he said, breaking the silence that had filled the car.

"I have a lot on my mind."

"Is part of what's on your mind my poor manners?"

She looked at him in surprise. "Perhaps," she admitted.

"I apologize for my flare of temper before we left. I just never expected my life to include being nursemaid to a lonely, ill-adjusted teenager."

"Lonely and ill-adjusted is a state of normalcy for most teenagers, and your apology is accepted." She gazed at him curiously. "Didn't you ever consider that you might one day be a father to a teenager?"

"My visions of the future never carried me past having a kid in diapers." His smile softened the tautness of his features, relaxed the lines around his mouth. "I thought about toddlers, even imagined Little League baseball and dance recitals, but I never thought about teenagers."

"How long were you married?"

"Five years."

"Your wife couldn't have children?"

His fingers tightened on the steering wheel, the knuckles turning white. "My wife wouldn't have children. She was afraid she'd lose the figure that allowed her to wear her favorite designer gowns. I think I grieved the loss of the opportunity to have children more than I mourned the end of my marriage." He cleared his throat. "What about you?"

"Jesse didn't hang around long enough for us to have a family. We married and divorced the same year."

"That's tough."

"Not really. In retrospect I think it would have been much tougher if Jesse had stuck around." She looked at her hands in her lap. "From the way it sounds, we really should introduce our exes to each other. They sound very compatible." She grinned and enjoyed the smile he offered back.

They fell silent, but it was not the same strained silence that had filled the car before. It was comfortable, companionable. Colleen wanted to ask him more questions, delve deeper into his past, learn more about the woman he'd loved more than life, but she didn't want to shatter the peace between them.

Soon they were in the city traffic. As they drew closer to the jewelry store, Colleen reached up and clasped the necklace tightly in her palm. She was afraid they were on a wild-goose chase.

She couldn't figure out what was so important about a necklace that people might break into her home to get it, that somebody would attack her in broad daylight and try to rip it from her neck. Still, she couldn't discount the coincidence of Caro's and Bonnie's necklaces being stolen.

By the time Gideon found a parking space within a block of Lowensteins, Colleen was a bundle of nerves. As they stepped out on the sidewalk, Gideon reached for her hand. "I want you to stay close. We can't take your safety for granted no matter where we are, until we get some answers." As his hand enclosed hers, he looked at her in surprise. "Your hand is like ice."

"I'm nervous," she admitted. "I keep wondering what the necklace has to do with anything. And is all this somehow connected to my father's death or Sam's disappearance?"

He squeezed her hand. "One step at a time, Colleen. First we need to find out everything we can about the necklace."

"I know. I just want this all over. I want Sam home and my life back to normal."

"And I want the New York Jets to win a Super Bowl." He smiled at her. "I guess we'll both have to wait and see what happens."

"Ah, the Giants will win long before the Jets," she replied.

He looked at her in surprise. "You a football fan?"

She nodded. "A rabid Giants fan."

The light conversation halted as they came to the door of Lowensteins Jewelry. Gideon released her hand and opened the door, and together they walked in.

Immediately they were approached by a smiling salesman. "Good afternoon," he said pleasantly. His sharp blue eyes behind his glasses took them both in. "Are we looking for something in particular today?" His smile widened. "Perhaps an engagement ring?"

Colleen felt a blush stain her cheeks. "Oh, no...we aren't...we don't..."

"We'd like to speak to a manager," Gideon cut in smoothly.

"I'm the manager. Jeffrey Rutherford, at your service," he replied.

"Mr. Rutherford, I suspect my father, Joseph Baker, bought this necklace from your store. We were wondering if you might possibly have any information about the transaction and the necklace." As Colleen spoke, she took off the piece of jewelry and handed it to Jeffrey Rutherford.

"Ah, a lovely piece," he said, then looked at Colleen sympathetically. "I knew your father well. He was a good man."

Colleen nodded and swallowed around the lump that rose in the back of her throat. "Yes, he was."

"I vaguely remember the day your father came in and ordered this. There was more than one, wasn't there?"

"Four. He bought four of them," Colleen replied.

"Please wait here and let me check my records." He handed Colleen the necklace then turned and disappeared into a back room.

"I can't imagine what he's going to be able to tell us that will help," Colleen said, a wave of helplessness sweeping over her. "I'm afraid this is all a wild-goose chase."

"Half of my work is chasing geese," Gideon returned with a smile. "All it takes is one goose to show the way to the golden egg."

"My problem is I think I've lost track of what the golden egg is." Colleen frowned. "At first the only thing I wanted was for Sam to come back. Now I want the real murderer found, I want to know who bugged my house. I want to know why somebody tried to tear that necklace off my neck." She broke off in frustration. "I sound like a whining child."

"We all need to whine once in a while," Gideon said. "At least you have very real reasons to whine." He put an arm around her and gave her a hug.

For a long moment Colleen remained in his embrace. Earlier when he had held her, she'd been too distraught to notice how very pleasant it was being in his arms. This time she reveled in the sensation.

They fit well together, as if their bodies were interlocking pieces of a puzzle. She felt safe in his arms, his familiar scent surrounding her and the warmth of his body suffusing her. She turned her head into the hollow of his neck, enjoying the soft scrape of whisker stubble against her face.

Jeffrey cleared his throat as he walked into the room. Reluctantly Colleen stepped out of Gideon's embrace.

"I'm not sure exactly what you're looking for," he said, his attention focused on some paperwork he held in his hands. "I can tell you the charms were specially made here in the store by one of our master jewelers."

"Could we speak to that jeweler?" Gideon asked.

Jeffrey looked pained. "I'm afraid that's quite impossible. The charms were made by Roger Wiley, and tragically, Mr. Wiley died a month ago in a freak car accident."

Colleen looked at Gideon, who frowned thoughtfully. "Could you possibly take a look at the bottom of the back of the charm and tell us what's engraved there?" Gideon asked.

"Certainly." Jeffrey disappeared once again into the back room, and reappeared a moment later with a jeweler's loupe. Taking the charm from Colleen, he studied the writing through the loupe. "Hmm, it isn't actual words, it appears to be a series of letters and numbers." He looked at Colleen once again. "You know, now I vaguely remember Roger telling me about these charms. If I recall correctly, your father had different numbers and letters engraved on the back of each charm, and he insisted Roger not keep a record of any kind." Jeffrey smiled sheepishly. "Roger found it quite odd and wondered if perhaps your father was under a lot of strain or something."

Gideon pulled a small notepad and a pen out of his pocket. "Can you read off those letters and numbers for me?"

"Certainly." Once again Jeffrey picked up the magnifying glass and the charm necklace. "M, P, 2, E, 6, C, V." As he read off each letter and number, Gideon wrote them down in his notebook.

"So what now?" Colleen asked moments later as she and Gideon got into the car.

"We need to figure out what these numbers and letters mean. They don't mean anything to you?"

"Nothing." Again despair swept through her. She sighed. "Somehow I feel like every day that passes, with every bit of new information we get, things only get more murky and confusing."

"My next concern is to find out the circumstances surrounding Roger Wiley's death."

Colleen looked at him in surprise. "Do you think his death has something to do with all this?" A renewed horror chilled her, and she wrapped her arms around herself.

"It just seems like another odd coincidence to me. A month ago Wiley dies in a freak accident. Three weeks ago somebody steals your sisters' necklaces, then yesterday somebody tries to take yours."

Put together, it sounded ominous. A shiver worked its way up Colleen's spine. "Gideon, I'm afraid," she said softly.

He started the car engine then turned and looked at her.

For a moment his gaze lingered on her, warm and soft. "Colleen, there are a lot of things I would never promise to you. But this, I promise. I intend to keep you safe from harm." His gaze lingered for another moment, this time hot and intense. He broke the gaze and put the car into gear.

Colleen looked at him for another long moment, a new, different kind of chill racing through her. Again she'd seen a hunger in his eyes.

As they headed toward Long Island, Colleen stared out the window, a new, disturbing though in her head. While he was protecting her from everyone else...who was going to protect her from him?

Chapter Eight

A charm, a series of numbers and a dead jeweler. Colleen stood at the bedroom window, staring out at the moonlight, trying to put it all together in her head. It had been two days since they'd been to the jewelry store, two additional days and nights at Gideon's.

Gideon had learned that Roger Wiley's car had been forced off the road by an unknown perpetrator. Unofficially it was being regarded as a murder. Unfortunately there had been no answers, no clues to let them know exactly what it all meant.

The charm necklace rested in a safety-deposit box at a nearby bank. Until they knew exactly why it was so important, they had agreed it was best to leave the necklace there.

Gideon had spent much of the past two days at the computer, linked onto various networks and hooked into different agencies, trying to figure out what the series of numbers on the back of the necklace meant. Each evening he'd been more frustrated than the last.

Eddy had been in and out, his awkward charm growing on Colleen with each encounter. In truth, she'd found his presence comforting, easing the subtle tension between Gideon and herself.

She turned away from the window, sleep even more elusive as her thoughts turned to Gideon. He was outside now, frustration evident as he paced the deck.

Gideon. He confused her as much as anything. There had been times in the past two days that she'd felt his gaze on her, thoughtful and probing. Other times his eyes had followed her hungrily, and she'd known he wanted her.

However, his desire frightened her because she didn't know what motivated it. Was he capable of separating the woman Colleen Baker from the status and money her name brought with it?

She should leave, go back to her duplex. Sooner or later she was going to have to return to her own life. It was possible Gideon might never be able to solve the mystery. She couldn't hide out here forever.

With this thought, knowing sleep would remain evasive, she left the room and walked out on the deck. Gideon saw her and smiled, his teeth shining in the full spill of moonlight. "We should start a new club... Insomniacs Are Us."

She smiled. "I have to admit, for the past couple of nights sleep has been a scarce commodity."

He unfolded two deck chairs. Sitting down in one, he motioned her to the other. "It's been my experience that sitting out here in the fresh air helps bring on sleepiness," he said as she sat next to him.

"I think it will take more than a little fresh air for me to get to sleep," she replied. "My mind keeps whirling with everything that's happened the last couple of days."

"I know what you mean." He leaned his head back and drew in a deep breath.

She settled back in the chair, an immediate peace sweeping over her as she drank in the majestic beauty of the moonlight on the water, heard the rhythmic swoosh of the waves, smelled the salt-tinged breeze that caressed her face like cool fingers. "Whatever made you decide to live on a houseboat?" she asked.

He stirred restlessly in his chair, his gaze on some point in the distance. "At the time I didn't have much choice on where I was going to live. I walked away from my marriage empty-handed and had just quit the police department. I had nothing, didn't know where I was going or what I intended to do. Of course, you wouldn't know about being broke, right?"

She shrugged. "There's different degrees of broke. When Jesse left me, my inheritance didn't bring me any comfort. When I was growing up without a mother, and with an absent father, I didn't feel like being wealthy was such a wonderful thing." She sighed and shifted positions on the chair. "I made the conscious decision to put most of my money in trust and live a normal life, surrounded by people who worked hard for their money." Smiling self-consciously, she waved her hands. "Besides, we weren't talking about me, we were talking about you and what brought you here."

He stirred restlessly, then stood up, leaned over the railing, and stared into the dark waters below. "I needed a place to stay for awhile, to regroup, decide where I was going with my life. This place belonged to a buddy of mine. He offered it to me as a temporary haven." He turned and smiled at her. "Somehow temporary became permanent. When I started making money as a private investigator, I decided to buy the boat." His smile turned reflective. "I feel safe here. The ocean is the one constant in my life, and it makes no demands on me, asks nothing from me."

Although his voice held no inflection, Colleen felt the pain beyond his words. It was the fear of a man who would risk nothing emotionally, who was willing only to bind himself to the uncaring, indifferent ocean waves. What had happened to him? What pain kept him so isolated?

Was her curiosity about him because she was a social worker and wanted to fix everyone's problems? Or was it because she cared about him on a more personal level? She consciously shifted away from these questions, unwilling to examine her feelings too closely.

"Did I put you to sleep?" he asked, a touch of dry humor in his tone.

"No, I was just thinking." She looked at him again, his features stark in the shafts of moonlight. "You told me the other night that you loved being a policeman. Why did you resign from the force?"

Again he was silent for a long moment, and his gaze went to the murky waters below the deck. "It's a long, ugly story," he finally answered.

"The night is long, and I'm not a bit sleepy," she answered.

He sighed. His features looked as if somehow he had swallowed all the darkness of the night. A muscle worked frantically in his jaw, and Colleen fought her impulse to tell him to forget it, she didn't want to know what dark secrets scarred his soul.

"In order to understand why I quit the police force, you have to understand a few things about my ex-wife." He swiped a hand through his hair and eased down in the chair next to Colleen.

"I was a police officer when I met Anne. She was shopping and had been mugged. I was the officer who responded to the incident. Although I thought she was beautiful, I knew she was wealthy and from a powerful family. I took the report, gave her my sympathy, then forgot all about it. Two days later she called me at the station, invited me out to dinner to show her appreciation for one of New York's finest."

His voice was curiously devoid of emotion, as if he was relating something that had little to do with him.

Still, Colleen could feel the tension that radiated from him, see the stress that tightened his features as he continued.

"I decided to go, first because I was curious about her, but mostly because I was flattered. At the time I didn't realize Anne always got what she wanted, and she had decided she wanted me." He laughed, a humorless sound that broke the peace of the night. "Anne was single-minded in her campaign to win me over, and eventually she did. I was crazy about her. We were married within six months."

He stood up again, as if needing the action of pacing to continue the story. "What I didn't understand when I married Anne was that she didn't want to be married to a cop. She'd married a sow's ear and wouldn't be satisfied until she turned me into a silk purse."

Colleen frowned. "I'm not sure I understand. What did she want you to do?"

"Join her father's company. Be a three-piece-suit man who spent my days making fortunes and my nights at thousand-dollar-a-plate charity functions. She couldn't understand that I couldn't do that...I'm simply not that kind of man. She hated my passion for my work, the long hours, the menial pay."

"And so you fought," Colleen replied.

Again he laughed hollowly. "Oh, how we fought. She insisted if I loved her, I'd quit the force. I maintained if she loved me, she'd never ask me to quit." He drew in a deep breath, then continued. "During this same time period, the department was undergoing an internal affairs investigation for corruption, rumors of cops on the take.''

He sat in the chair, his shoulders slumped forward as if in defeat. He looked at her, and in the depths of his eyes she saw the whisper of vulnerability, realized that by telling her all this he was trusting her with a precious piece of himself. ''I never knew she'd go so far.'' His voice was a mere whisper. ''I was so caught up in loving her, still so amazed that she'd married me, I didn't realize how far she'd go to get what she wanted. I didn't see it coming at all.''

Colleen swallowed hard, realizing her mouth had gone dry. She wanted to wrap him in her arms, hold him tight. She didn't want to hear any more and yet knew she had to finish what she had begun. She licked her lips, dread coursing through her. ''What did she do?'' she finally asked.

''Internal Affairs called me in, told me they had found a bank account in my name. The account had more money in it than I could make in a lifetime of being a policeman, and I'd always been quite verbal in the fact that when I married Anne I insisted we keep our money separate.''

''They thought you were on the take?'' Colleen asked incredulously.

He held out his hands and shrugged. ''What else could they think? Although they were honest enough to tell me with my connection to Anne they didn't want to prosecute, they did recommend highly that I leave the force."

"Oh, Gideon," she said softly, her heart aching for him.

"And so I resigned from the force." He leaned back in the chair, his body less tense than before. She was surprised when he smiled and shook his head. "You want to hear the most incredible part of all? When I confronted Anne about it, she admitted that she and her father had opened the account, hoping what had happened would happen. She genuinely didn't understand why I was so mad. It was at that moment I realized I didn't love her, couldn't ever love her again."

Colleen tasted his betrayal, suddenly understood why he kept himself so isolated. His wife had not only betrayed him on a personal level, she'd destroyed him on a professional level, all in the name of love. Was it any wonder that he maintained he would never love again?

"Gideon, I'm so sorry," she finally said. She reached out and placed a hand on his arm, wanting to connect with him, somehow ease the pains of his past. "I just get the feeling that you've shut yourself off from people because you've been hurt in the past. I...I hate to see that."

He looked at her in wry amusement. "Ah, your profession is showing, Ms. Jensen. I can see you frothing at the mouth with anticipation of somehow rehabilitating me."

She snatched her hand away from his arm, stung by the taunting sarcasm in his voice. "Maybe my concern has nothing to do with my profession," she snapped. "Did you ever consider my concern might just be that of one person for another?" She stood up. "I think I'll go to bed. Suddenly sleep sounds very appealing." She turned to leave, then gasped as he grabbed her by the arm and twirled her around to face him once again.

"Are you saying you care about me?" He stood so close to her she could feel the heat from his body, and his breath fanned her face. He reached up, and with the tip of one finger touched her lips ever so gently. "Tell me, Colleen. Just how far are you willing to go to rehabilitate me?"

"I—I..." The power of speech left her as he pulled her tightly against the length of his body. His eyes stared into hers with an intensity that stole her breath away. Before she could protest or pull away, his mouth descended to hers.

Greedily his mouth plied hers with heat. His arms were tight, holding her captive against him. A willing captive, for she made no attempt to escape, to leave his embrace.

Instead, she welcomed him, opening her mouth, wanting to deepen the intimacy of the kiss. She didn't consider the utter foolishness of kissing Gideon, didn't consider his motivation in wanting to kiss her. She only wanted to experience the moment, savor each exquisite sensation that rippled through her as his mouth possessed hers.

As his tongue dipped inside her mouth, she felt as if she'd swallowed the moon and the stars. Why else the explosion of warmth within her?

She reached up and stroked the side of his face, enjoying the rough feel of whisker stubble beneath her fingertips. Her other hand went to the nape of his neck, her fingers entwining in the richness of his hair.

He moaned deep in his throat as she pressed herself intimately against him, unsure what exactly she wanted from him, but wanting more. His mouth left hers, instead trailing hot kisses behind her ear, along the side of her neck.

His hands moved up and down her back, at first softly, then gradually with more pressure. She dropped her head back, allowing his mouth access to the tender area of her throat. She gasped as one of his hands moved from her back, around to the ribs just below her breasts.

His hand covered her breast as his mouth once again claimed hers. Through the silky material of her pajamas, her nipple stiffened toward the warmth of his caress, and Colleen wanted his caress on her without the barrier of the material.

As if he could read her mind and shared her desire, his fingers nimbly worked to unbutton her top. As he unfastened the last button, there was a brief moment when Colleen felt the cool night breeze on her bare skin, then the coolness was replaced by the warmth of his hand.

It had been so long...so long since Colleen had felt desired. It felt so good to be held in masculine arms, to feel the beat of his heart mirroring the frantic pace of her own. Someplace in the back of her mind, she knew the pleasure was not in being held in any masculine arms, but distinctly in being held by Gideon.

"Gideon." She said his name softly. "Make love to me."

He froze, his eyes locked with hers. She watched the passion die from their dark depths, replaced by an unpleasant gleam that made her stiffen defensively. "Is that how far you're willing to go to reform me?" A dark eyebrow shot up mockingly. "I don't know...it might work. You're wealthy like Anne was. You come from the same kind of background. Maybe in using your body without loving you I'll feel like I'm paying back those who hurt me."

She gasped at the cruelty of his words. "I'm not Anne."

His eyes darkened, and gently he pulled the edges of her pajama top together. He sighed, the heavy expulsion of breath a sound of defeat. "Go to bed, Colleen. I think we're both in over our heads."

Over their heads? Colleen felt as if she was drowning in emotion. She looked at him for another long moment, then, turning, she went inside.

Once in her room, she turned off the light and got into bed, her body aching with unfulfillment. Her face burned as she remembered her wanton response to him. How quickly, how easily he had managed to make her forget everything but him.

She had to leave here. She didn't care what kind of danger she might encounter by moving back to the duplex. Nothing was as dangerous to her well-being as Gideon. She closed her eyes, needing the darkness to acknowledge what was in her heart. Somehow, some-way, in the brief time she had known Gideon Graves, she had managed to fall hopelessly, irrevocably in love with him.

Gideon was awake before the morning light illuminated the eastern sky. He sat on the deck chair, sipping a cup of coffee, watching as the first tendrils of light peeked over the horizon.

He'd slept little all night, instead tossing and turning on the uncomfortable sofa while his head played and replayed those moments of holding Colleen in his arms.

He'd intentionally been unkind, needing to alienate her, not only for her own sake but for his, as well. She needed him at the moment, needed his expertise to help her find Sam, help her muddle through the mystery darkening her life. But he knew once that need had dissipated she would go on with a life that wouldn't, couldn't include him.

Different worlds, different backgrounds, and he couldn't trust his feelings to know if he would be using Colleen to assuage the sins of Anne.

Anne. He drained his coffee cup and placed it on the floor next to his chair. He rose and walked to the railing. Leaning against it, his thoughts returned to his ex-wife. Funny, when he'd spoken of her last night with Colleen, he'd realized that at some point he'd lost his bitterness, moved past it.

He felt good about that, as if somehow he'd grown. Still, he wasn't fool enough to want to repeat the experience, and that's what he feared he would do with Colleen. Oh, he didn't believe she was devious like Anne had been. But she would have expectations, and sooner or later he would disappoint her.

"Good morning."

He jumped in surprise at the sound of her voice. He turned to see her standing in the doorway. She'd obviously been up for some time as she was dressed and had her overnight bag in her hand.

"Good morning," he replied, shoving away a small tinge of shame as he remembered the way they had parted the night before, the stark cruelty of his words to her.

"I think perhaps it's time I go home." Her face was devoid of expression, making it impossible for him to know how she felt. "The necklace is safe for now, and I can't hide out here forever. I need to get back to work, to my own life."

On the one hand he wanted to sigh in relief and shove her out the door. On another note he knew it was risky for her to return before they at least knew the importance of the necklace. "We don't have any answers yet," he said.

"I can't put my life on hold until I get answers," she returned. "Besides—" her gaze skittered away from his "—I just think it best if I go home."

"This is about last night, isn't it?"

Her face colored slightly. "Don't be ridiculous. This has nothing to do with last night." She gripped her bag tighter against her side. "I've already called for a taxi. It should be here any minute."

"I would have driven you home."

She shrugged. "I didn't want to be a bother. Besides, I wanted to get home early enough so I can have a locksmith out. I'm installing all new locks on the doors."

He nodded. "A wise move. I know the house is clean at the moment. My friend removed all the listening devices."

In the distance a horn honked. They both turned to see the yellow cab waiting in the parking lot. She looked at Gideon, her eyes expressionless. "You'll continue working on the case?"

"You'll continue to pay me?"

This brought another flush of color to her cheeks. "Of course," she replied. "And thank you for your hospitality." She started down the dock, then hesitated and turned to him. "You'll call me?"

He nodded, watching until she disappeared into the cab and the cab drove out of sight. He had a feeling he could have stopped her, that had he insisted she stay for safety reasons she probably would have reluctantly agreed. However, he knew Colleen was resourceful, and now that she knew she might be at risk, she would do whatever she needed to keep herself safe.

It was better this way. He'd nearly lost control with her last night. He'd wanted her so badly it had hurt. He'd wanted to lose himself in the smoky depths of her eyes, forget his past, not worry about the future. He'd simply wanted to make love to Colleen. And, oh, what a mistake that would have been.

He'd sworn to himself he would never be vulnerable to a woman again. He'd sworn he would never care again. Yes, better she was gone and no longer a constant, daily temptation.

He bent over and picked up his coffee cup from the deck, fighting off a sudden desire for a cigarette. Funny, during the time Colleen had been at the houseboat, he hadn't felt the need for a smoke, had even given up chewing on licorice.

Frowning, he went into the house and poured himself a fresh cup of coffee. The silence surrounded him, heavy and oppressive. There was no remnant of Colleen. Even the air itself no longer contained the sweet scent of her. Instead it was flat and stale.

He moved over to the window and stared out, a tinge of relief flowing through him as he saw Eddy walking toward the boat. For the first time he looked forward to Eddy's company. For the first time in three years, he didn't want to be alone.

Chapter Nine

"Want to go to lunch?" Margie peered into Colleen's office.

Colleen gestured to the files strewn across the top of her desk. "Better not. As usual, I'm behind."

Margie grinned slyly. "You'd get more work done if you didn't spend so much time staring off into space." She paused a moment, gazing at Colleen in speculation. "If I didn't know you better, I'd think you were lovesick."

"Don't be silly," Colleen scoffed, inwardly cursing the blush that warmed her cheeks. "I've just had so much on my mind the last couple of days."

"Did you get that security system installed?" Margie asked.

Colleen nodded. "They finished it yesterday. I feel like I'm living in Fort Knox."

"If you feel safe, that's all that's important." Margie looked at her watch. "I'm going to scoot out and get a sandwich. I'll lock the door as I leave, and I'll be back in about thirty minutes." With a wiggle of fingers, Margie left Colleen's doorway, and a moment later Colleen heard the main office door open and close.

Leaning back in her chair, Colleen closed her eyes and expelled a deep, weary sigh. It had been two days since she'd left the houseboat, and in those two days she'd had all the locks on the duplex changed and a full security system installed. She felt safe again...safe and alone.

She got up from her desk and went to the window, staring out in the direction of the marina. Gideon. There had been few minutes in the past two days that he hadn't been on her mind, in her heart.

She'd heard nothing from him, assumed he was no closer to finding the whereabouts of Sam than he had been on the day she'd hired him. Although disappointed, she wasn't surprised by the lack of clues. She was beginning to realize that the quest to find Sam had been an obsession because there was nothing else in her life. When her father had been murdered and Sam had disappeared, Colleen had put what personal life she had on hold.

More than that, she had begun to realize that in the space of time after her divorce from Jesse and before the murder of her father, she had leaned too heavily on Sam. She'd used her brother and his family to fill up the lonely spaces inside her. It had taken her feelings for Gideon to make her realize how empty her life had been.

Turning away from the window, she sighed again. Margie had been right. She was lovesick. She was sick from loving a man incapable of returning her love.

Remembering Gideon's caresses that last night created a bittersweet pain in her heart. At least he'd been honest with her. He'd never pretended to want anything more than her fee. He'd been truthful in telling her he might like making love to her, not because he loved her, but to somehow get back at the ex-wife who'd hurt him.

"Colleen, you have a miserable penchant for falling in love with the wrong man," she said aloud. Returning to her desk, she shoved the thought aside and instead focused her attention on the files in front of her.

She'd only been working a few minutes when she heard a light rap on the outer office door. Assuming it was Margie returning from lunch, she hurried to let her in.

"Oh," she squeaked in surprise as she opened the door and saw Gideon standing in the midday sunshine. "I thought you were Margie."

"Nah. She's shorter than me and wears more dresses."

Colleen laughed, trying to ignore the burst of warmth that radiated through her as she gazed at him. "What are you doing here? Do you have something for me?"

"More questions." The smile that had initially curved his lips when she opened the door disappeared behind a frown.

"Come on into my office." As he stepped inside, she carefully locked the outer door behind him.

"I'm glad to see you're being careful, playing it safe." His eyes were dark, emotionless, making her wonder if she'd only imagined the passion glazing them that last night she'd been at his houseboat.

She nodded, schooling her thoughts to the here and now. "I've also had a security system installed at the duplex," she said as she led him into her private office.

He sank down in the chair directly in front of her desk and waited for her to get settled. "I'm sorry to say I have nothing to report on Sam, although I've managed to obtain copies of police reports and now know that at one time he was in Casey's Corners, Kansas. There hasn't been a sighting or a clue where he might have gone after that."

Colleen shoved the files on her desk to one side, unsurprised by his words. "I just wish I knew where he was, what he was doing."

"Well, being wanted for murder is a pretty compelling reason for staying in hiding," Gideon observed dryly.

"I think it goes beyond that. I really believe if that was the only thing going on, Sam would be here, fighting to clear his name." She leaned back in the chair thoughtfully. "Sam isn't a coward. He faces his problems, his feelings, head-on. He wouldn't run just because he's wanted by the police. There has to be something else going on." She focused her attention on Gideon. "You said you had some questions?"

He nodded. "I haven't been able to get those letters and numbers on the back of your necklace out of my mind. I've checked for safety-deposit boxes, secret bank accounts...but nothing indicates what those numbers are for. They've got to mean something, and I've racked my brain trying to figure it out." He leaned forward in the chair, his brow furrowed in thought.

Colleen fought her impulse to shove her chair back, away from his familiar scent. What she really wanted to do was fall into his arms, tell him she didn't care if he wanted her money. It didn't matter if he wanted to use her for his own brand of revenge. She just wanted him to hold her, kiss her, pretend to love her for a moment.

She stood up, angry with herself and her thoughts. "So, what have you come up with?"

"I'd like to take a look at your father's personal papers, financial records, anything that might give us a clue as to what those numbers and letters mean. Surely your father left records behind. Do you know where they might be? Who might have them now?"

Colleen frowned. "I imagine most of those things are still in Daddy's apartment. Initially the police wanted to see everything, but they returned it. I believe Carolyn put them all back in the apartment."

"Your father had an apartment? I thought he had an estate in the Hamptons."

"He does. That's our family home. But he also kept an apartment in Manhattan, not far from the Baker Enterprises headquarters." She paused, feeling his tension as he stood up.

"Can you take me there? Do you have a key to get in?"

"Sure, I have a key. When do you want to go?"

"As soon as possible. Now."

"I can't go now," she protested. "It's the middle of the workday." She bent over her desk and studied her afternoon schedule. "I could get away by three."

"I'll pick you up then."

As he walked out of her office, she followed close behind, half resenting the fact that he could be so professional, so coolly detached from her. As they reached the main door, he turned to her. "It might be wise if you don't wait for me on the bench outside."

"Don't worry. I never make the same mistake twice," she said dryly.

"Three o'clock," he reminded her, then turned and walked away.

She watched him until he disappeared from her view. She closed the door and locked it, her heart aching with the weight of her love. She'd lied when she told him she didn't make mistakes twice. Twice in her lifetime, she'd managed to fall in love with men who apparently didn't have the capacity to love her back.

Gideon decided to go to the houseboat and wait for three o'clock to arrive. He was anxious to see Joseph Baker's personal papers. Somehow, he knew the necklaces were tied to the murder and therefore to Sam's disappearance.

Eddy was waiting for him, sitting on one of the deck chairs. He stood up as Gideon approached, as usual his face lit with a full smile. "Hey, Gideon," he greeted cheerfully. "Been working the case?"

"Sort of," Gideon answered, unsurprised when Eddy followed him inside. He went directly to the refrigerator and grabbed a beer. Popping the top, he sat down at the table, wishing Eddy away, wanting the next couple hours alone to mentally prepare himself for spending time with Colleen.

"So, what have you got lined up for me to do?" Eddy asked as he slid into the seat opposite Gideon.

Gideon took a deep swallow of beer and gazed at Eddy in irritation. "Don't you have any friends your own age? Surely you can find something better to do than hang out here with me."

Eddy's smile wavered in uncertainty. "But I like hanging out here with you."

Frustration gnawed at Gideon. The frustration of choices he had made, easy decisions that had required no courage, choices that had kept him safe, isolated and without emotional risk. "Look around Eddy. Is this what you want for yourself—the kind of life I lead?" He slammed his beer can on the table, causing Eddy to jump in surprise. "You want to spend your days delving into other people's lives because you have no life of your own? You want to live on a half-sinking boat because you don't know when your next pay is coming in or how far it will have to stretch?"

"But, Gideon . . . I think you're great," Eddy said, his ears pinkened by the confession.

"Go home, Eddy," Gideon replied flatly. "Go home and figure out a way to make a success of your life." He ran a hand through his hair and looked at the kid, who stared at him with adoring eyes. He jerked up from his chair and went to the window, his back to the boy still seated at the table. "Don't try to be like me, Eddy. Be better than me."

"But, Gideon . . ."

He whirled around to face the teenager. "Let me tell you the truth about Gideon Graves. You probably haven't heard, but they call me the fallen angel of Long Island. I was asked to leave the police force because they thought I was a dirty cop. I decided to be a private investigator because I don't know how to do anything else. I'm a loser, Eddy, not a role model. Now get the hell out of here, and don't come back."

Eddy jumped up from the table, his face ashen. "I'll go, Gideon," he said, his voice trembling as he backed toward the door. "I don't want to be a bother. But you should know, I heard the story about you a long time ago. I didn't believe it when I first heard it, and I don't believe it now. There's no way you were a dirty cop.'' Without waiting for Gideon's reply, he turned and ran out the door.

Gideon fought his impulse to run after him, knowing this was for the best. Eddy needed to think of his future, and the future was filled with golden opportunities for an enthusiastic, bright teen. Eddy's future couldn't be found here, and Gideon cared too deeply about the kid to allow him to remain. Better this way. Better Eddy hate him and move on with his life.

As he moved to the kitchen table, once again the silence surrounded him, engulfed him. He remained seated at the table until it was time to meet Colleen.

As he drove to the social services office, he once again turned the mystery of the necklaces over in his mind. He hoped they would find some answers hidden in Joseph Baker's private papers.

He consciously refused to think about Colleen, unwilling to analyze his feelings where she was concerned. He didn't want to remember how right she had felt in his arms, didn't want to dwell on how quickly she had responded to his touch, how passionately she'd returned his kisses. He didn't want to think about how desperately he'd wanted to make love to her.

Passion, that's all he felt for her. Passion and desire. It was only natural. After all, it had been a little over three years since he'd been with a woman. His desire had been on hold for too long. It was no wonder she'd managed to spark a flame inside him. Any attractive woman would have probably been able to do the same thing.

Maybe it was time he found some flashy bimbo. He smiled humorlessly as he remembered Colleen telling him that was probably his type of woman. "I wonder if Magnum ever had these problems," he muttered irritably as he pulled his car against the curb in front of Colleen's office building.

He didn't even have time to shut off the engine before she came out. He tightened his hands on the steering wheel as he saw the way the late afternoon sunshine shone in her hair, picking up mahogany highlights he hadn't noticed before. She opened the passenger door and slid inside, bringing with her the sweet scent of flowers and flashing a length of nylon-clad leg.

"Where to?" he asked curtly.

"Central Park," she replied as she fastened her seat belt.

He pulled away from the curb and for the next half hour neither of them spoke. That's one thing Gideon had to give her—unlike some women, she knew the value of silence, didn't seem to have a compulsion to fill each space with meaningless conversation.

Still, as the silence lingered it seemed to grow, filling the car. He cast a glance in her direction, wondering what she was thinking. Her face was turned toward the passenger window, giving him only the view of her profile. The sun streaming in the window painted her features with a lustrous golden light. His stomach clenched and his hands tightened on the steering wheel.

"Busy afternoon?" he finally said, unable to stand the silence any longer.

"Worse than some, better than others," she replied. She stirred in the seat, finally turned to face him. "I guess you had a busy afternoon."

He looked at her in surprise. "What makes you think so?"

"Eddy came to see me."

Although there was no censure in her words, no judgment at all, a burst of shame shot through Gideon. "It was time the kid heard some hard truths," he said defensively.

She stared at him for a long moment. "It's a shame you can see the truth in everything but yourself."

"What's that supposed to mean?" he asked brusquely.

She shook her head. "Never mind, Gideon. Eddy will be fine. He loves you, and nothing you can do or say to him will change that." She looked out the window. "Don't worry, his love doesn't cost you a thing, either financially or emotionally."

A vast, hollow emptiness swept through him at her words. He felt the need to say something, but no words formed in his head. He didn't know how to answer.

The silence grew once again, accompanying them for the remainder of the ride. The traffic was heavy, further increasing the knot of tension in Gideon's stomach. Colleen navigated him into the private underground parking area of the lush apartment building overlooking Central Park.

"None of us has been here since just after Daddy's funeral," she said as they rode up the elevator to the nineteenth floor.

He hadn't considered how difficult coming here might be for her. Stress lined her face, making her look fragile, vulnerable, and he fought the impulse to gather her in his arms. "Are you okay with this?"

She hesitated a moment, then nodded. "Yes. I just hope we find some answers here."

When they reached the apartment, she unlocked the door and drew a deep breath. Stale air greeted them as they walked inside.

Colleen immediately went to the windows and opened the curtains to let in the early evening sunshine. As she did that, Gideon looked around with interest. It was obvious the apartment had been left undisturbed for a long time. Dust covered the tops of the wooden furniture, and there was a general aura of abandonment.

"Why have you all kept this place?" he asked.

Colleen turned from the window, her gaze darting around the room as if she'd never seen it before. "I'm not sure. Daddy spent more time here than anyplace else." She sank down on the maroon and navy striped sofa. "For a long time it was too painful to think about coming here and sorting through his personal things. It was easier to just pay the rent each month."

She got up and walked over to a handsome bookcase where dozens of leather-bound books were neatly aligned. "Daddy collected books, but I never saw him take the time to relax and read. He worked too hard, probably figured one day he'd retire and have time to do all the things he wanted to do."

Turning to Gideon, she drew in a deep breath and swallowed hard. She looked fragile, with the sheen of tears in her eyes and her lower lip trembling with emotion. "Come on, let's get this over with," she said.

Beckoning him to follow, she led him into a huge bedroom. On the large desk that occupied one portion of one wall sat a computer. Nearby on the floor was a large box of paperwork.

"These are all Daddy's records," Colleen said as she lifted the box off the floor and onto the desk top. "I can't imagine what can possibly be in here to help us. The police had all this stuff and didn't find anything they thought related to the murder."

"But the police didn't know about the necklaces," Gideon reminded her. He pointed to the computer. "May I?"

She nodded, standing behind him as he sat at the desk and turned on the computer. More than anything Gideon wanted some answers and was surprised to realize he didn't want them for himself. He wanted answers for Colleen.

Minutes passed as Gideon worked on the computer, checking directories, calling up files, trying to find something, anything to relate why Joseph Baker had bought four necklaces and had numbers and letters engraved on the backs.

While he worked, he was conscious of Colleen as she walked around the room, pacing behind him. Never could he remember being so attuned to the nuances of a woman, the sound of her breathing, the whispered rustle of her clothing, the tiny sighs that escaped her from time to time.

The evening sunlight disappeared and she turned on the lights to ward off the darkness of night. It was nearly eight o'clock when Gideon discovered a hidden file.

"Colleen, there's a file here that isn't named," he said, trying to keep his excitement out of his voice.

She walked over and stood directly behind him, a hand on his shoulder. "What does that mean?"

"It could be nothing, it could be something," he hedged, trying to ignore the pleasure and warmth of her touch.

She laughed. "Well, thanks for that, Sherlock Holmes."

He grinned at her, then focused his attention on the screen. "Okay, it could mean several things. Perhaps your father accidently forgot to name a file, or maybe he intentionally hid it."

She leaned down, her face so close to his he knew if he turned his head his lips could touch her. "So, how do you retrieve a hidden file?" she asked.

"By calling it by name."

She frowned. "But we don't know the name."

"And that's the problem." Gideon kept his gaze carefully schooled on the screen before him. "Let's try a few names." He typed in Joseph, Sam, Carolyn, Bonnie, Colleen, anything they could think of that Joseph might have used. Nothing worked.

"Try necklace and charm," Colleen prompted.

Gideon typed in the words, but still nothing happened. "No good," he said in frustration.

"How about phoenix?" she asked.

Gideon typed in the word and gasped in surprise as the screen darkened, then a picture of the mythical bird appeared. "Bingo." He breathed softly as Colleen's fingers tensed on his shoulder. Across the bottom of the screen, the word *password* flashed. "I know what the numbers and letters are for on the back of the charms," he said.

"What?"

He leaned back in the chair and rubbed his eyes tiredly. "They're the code for entering this file."

Colleen frowned. "But we don't have all the charms, so we don't have all the code. Isn't there some other way to get into the file?"

"There could be a back door, but I don't know enough to access it, and I don't know what kind of protections your father might have written into this particular program."

"So what do we do now?" Colleen asked.

"We take the hard drive to my place. I've got a friend who's a computer whiz. If anyone can find a way into this file, he can."

It took Gideon only a few minutes to load up what they needed and take it to the car. When he returned, Colleen was drawing the draperies closed and turning off the lights.

As he stepped out in the hallway, Colleen lingered just inside the apartment. "I've got to call Carolyn and Bonnie. It's time we clean all this out and let the apartment go." She closed the door and locked it, for a moment leaning heavily against the ornate wood. "Daddy is never coming back here, and it's time for us to stop pretending he will."

She turned and faced Gideon, sadness reflected in her eyes. "And it's possible Sam might never return."

The impulse Gideon had fought all day swept over him once more. This time he didn't fight it, but rather followed it, stepping forward and gathering her into his arms.

She leaned into him, her head resting on his shoulder, her breath warming the side of his neck. Gideon closed his eyes, memorizing the way her body molded to his, the way her scent swirled in his head.

He loved her, and his feelings for her had nothing to do with Anne. They were separate from any silly kind of revenge, removed from mere physical desire. He ached with her sadness, knew he would sing with her joy. Yes, somehow in the craziness that he called his life, he'd fallen in love with Colleen Baker Jensen.

In the best of worlds, he wanted to find Sam for her, gift her with what she professed to want most. More than anything, Gideon wanted to be her hero. But he knew that wasn't possible. This wasn't the best of worlds, and if he couldn't give her Sam, he would do the next best thing he could for her. He would walk out of her life forever.

Chapter Ten

They were quiet on the ride to the duplex, although it wasn't the same strained silence they'd endured on the way into the city. Instead Colleen felt a weary kind of resignation and realized it was time to stop chasing the elusive shadow of Sam, time to move ahead with her life. She felt as if she'd been in a holding pattern since Sam's disappearance. It was time to move forward.

She looked at Gideon, wondering if there was a place for him in her future. He confused her. He professed to need nobody, had warned her that if he slept with her it wouldn't mean anything. And yet his touch spoke different words, the tender way he held her communicated emotions much different than those he mouthed.

Who was the real Gideon Graves? The tough, burned-out ex-cop who was most comfortable alone? Or was it the man who had allowed a lonely teenager to hang out at his place for the past three years, a man who seemed to know instinctively when she needed to be held? She knew which one was real. She wasn't sure he knew. Leaning her head against the seat, she closed her eyes, allowing the motion of the car to lull her.

"Colleen, you're home."

She opened her eyes as Gideon pulled into her driveway. "Oh, sorry, I must have nodded off." Straightening up in the seat, she looked at him. "Gideon, would you mind coming inside for a few minutes? I've got something I'd like to talk to you about." She hadn't realized until this moment that she intended to put an end to their business relationship.

When he received his fee from her, would there be anything left between them? Would he take his money and run? Never see her again? Never hold her again? She was afraid of the answer, yet had to know.

"I wouldn't turn down a cup of coffee," he replied as he shut off the car engine.

Together they got out of the car and walked to the porch, where Colleen spied a paper bag sitting on the stoop. "Ah, you're in luck," she exclaimed as she saw the note from Elda. "Cinnamon knots, compliments of Elda."

"I wonder if your neighbor ever thought about taking up residence on a houseboat," Gideon said as he followed her inside the house.

"I'll share these only if you promise you won't try to steal Elda away," she exclaimed. "Have a seat, and I'll get the coffee going." She smiled at him as she carried the sweets into the kitchen with her.

It took only minutes for her to make the coffee and arrange the sweets on a platter. When she went into the living room, Gideon was seated on the sofa, thumbing through a family photo album.

"It must have been nice, growing up with brothers and sisters," he said as he closed the album and set it where it had been on the coffee table.

"Yes, it was nice," Colleen agreed. "Although to be perfectly honest, Bonnie and Carolyn and I weren't that close until we got older."

He smiled at her. "Must have been tough to be the youngest of four."

"Sometimes, but I managed to survive." She handed him his cup of coffee and set the platter of cinnamon knots on the table in front of him.

"You've had to survive a number of tragedies," he said, his voice warm with a hint of admiration. "I'll bet you're a good social worker."

"I try to be. It's important to me." She sat down near him. "My father was horrified when I announced I was going into social work. He'd assumed I'd go into the family business. He didn't understand how important it was for me to establish my own identity, separate from the Baker name and fortune."

"I'd say you've managed to do that. You seem quite content with the life you've made for yourself."

Colleen nodded thoughtfully. "Yes, for the most part I'm happy, although there's always room for improvement." She couldn't tell him about the loneliness that ate at her, the nights she wished for somebody to hold her close, whisper love words in her ears.

Gideon leaned back on the sofa, looking so at ease, so much at home, Colleen's heart ached. "So, what did you want to talk to me about?" he asked as he reached for one of the sweets.

She drew in a deep breath. "I hired you while we were having cinnamon knots and coffee. I guess we've sort of come full circle," she said softly, watching his expression as he fully comprehended her words.

His eyes narrowed. "You're firing me?"

"No, Gideon, I'm not firing you," she denied quickly, then sighed again. "I've just realized that I should have never hired you in the first place. Sam doesn't want to be found, and I've already wasted too much time on a wild-goose chase." She stared into her coffee cup. "My obsession with Sam is over. I have to face the fact that I might never know what happened to him. It's time for me to move on."

He nodded, his eyes as dark, as fathomless as her coffee. "I think you're wise. It is time for you to move on."

His words caused a flicker of pain inside her heart, as she had the distinct impression he wasn't only speaking of her getting past her obsession with Sam, but also moving beyond him.

She opened her purse and withdrew her check-book, trying to keep her hand steady as she wrote out a check for what she owed him.

As she handed him the check his eyes remained hooded, emotionless. He folded it up and put it in his pocket, then reached for another cinnamon knot. "One for the road," he said as he stood up.

"You don't have to run off," she protested, wanting him to stay just a little bit longer, not ready to say goodbye.

"Oh, I think I do." He started for the door, and Colleen ran after him, realizing she couldn't let him walk away without telling him what was in her heart.

"Gideon, please. Wait."

He turned and looked at her, for a moment a whisper of pain reflected in his eyes. It was enough to give Colleen the nerve to tell him how she felt. "Please," she repeated, moving to stand directly before him. His eyes were blank again, inviting no heartfelt confession, but still she forged ahead. "Gideon, I don't want you to leave here and never see me again."

"You know where I live if you ever need a good private investigator," he answered flippantly.

"You know that's not what I mean." She reached out and grabbed his shirtsleeve, holding tight.

"Colleen . . . don't," he said softly, his expression one of pain.

"Don't what?" For some reason, she felt a flicker of anger rise inside her.

"Whatever it is you're about to say... please don't say it."

She released her hold on his shirt. "Why? Because you don't want to hear it?" She gazed at him searchingly, loving his intractable hair that refused to stay combed, the strength of his jawline with its fine whisker stubble, the mouth that looked so strong and unyielding but was as soft as velvet on hers. "Gideon, I have to say it."

He swept a hand through his hair, averting his gaze from hers. "Okay, what is it?"

"I love you."

He closed his eyes for a moment, his body tense, hands balled into fists at his side. Then he looked at her, the dark depths of his eyes as turbulent as a night storm on the sea. "And what do you expect me to do about it?"

"Absolutely nothing." She swallowed hard against the futile tears that burned her eyes. "I told you once before, Gideon. My love is free. No expectations, no responsibilities come with it. It's a gift."

"I don't want your gift," he replied, anger building in his voice. "How in the hell could you let this happen?"

"Believe me, I'm not happy about the situation, either," she replied dryly. "But I couldn't let you just walk out of my life forever without at least telling you how I feel." She walked closer to him, close enough to see the golden flecks in the irises of his eyes.

He backed away from her and raked a trembling hand through his hair. "Colleen, I'm sorry if I somehow led you on. But I think I've been very honest with you from the beginning. I intend to live my life alone. I don't need anyone. I don't want anybody's love. I'm not good for anyone."

She reached up and placed her palm on the side of his face. "Oh, Gideon, you're such a good man. Why can't you see that for yourself?"

He took her hand in his, removed it from his face. "Colleen, I'm not a hero. Hell, I couldn't even find Sam for you." Frustration twisted his features and a muscle worked frantically in his jaw.

"I don't care about that anymore. I don't want a hero. I don't need a hero in my life. I only need you. I want you, and you can't tell me you don't care about me." Her heart pounded frantically in her chest as he turned once again to leave. Anger ripped through her. "That's it, Gideon, run. Run like you have been doing for the last three years."

He froze with his back to her, his hand poised over the doorknob. Colleen swiped angrily at the tears that tracked down her cheeks. "Run back to your boat where you can wallow in self-pity, alienate yourself from any form of love at all." She gasped for breath, then continued, "You have two people who see all your faults and love you in spite of them. You've already tried to shove Eddy out of your life. Now you want to do the same to me."

For a long moment he remained frozen, and hope filled Colleen's heart. "Goodbye, Colleen," he finally said, then he turned the knob, opened the door and walked away.

Colleen stared at the space where he had been, an emptiness inside her so intense it nearly stole her breath away. He was gone, and she would probably never see him again. She felt as if she'd lost something precious, something she should have never been so foolish to want. She sank down on the sofa, a hole in her chest where her heart had been. She'd lied to him when she'd told him that her love was free. She had wanted something from him in return. She'd wanted him to love her back.

Gideon sat on his deck, watching the sun descend on another day. A week had gone by since he'd said goodbye to Colleen. A long, lonely week of too much thought, too much rumination, too many regrets.

His first regret had been in not fighting the police department for his job three years before. At the time he'd been so sick about Anne's betrayal, he'd rolled over and played dead. He'd been innocent and should have demanded a full-scale investigation.

His second regret was more complicated. Eddy. He hadn't realized how much he cared about the kid until this past week, when Eddy hadn't been around at all. He hadn't realized how the kid's adulation had soothed old wounds, buoyed his spirits. He hadn't been willing to admit that it felt good to look after

Eddy, listen to his chatter, be infected with his enthusiasm for life in general.

Gideon certainly didn't lament the fact that he'd told Eddy to find a decent future, be a better man than Gideon was. However, what he did regret was how he had told Eddy those things. He should have never done it in anger. He should have done it with love.

And that brought him to his final regret. Colleen.

He leaned his head back and closed his eyes with a sigh. Immediately his mind conjured up a slide show, portraits of Colleen from the first moment he'd seen her standing in his doorway with the sun at her back, to the final night when he'd told her goodbye and tears had trailed down her cheeks. Her beauty touched him, her courage and spirit inspired him. Her love amazed him.

He sighed again, realizing he was building a lifetime of regrets.

"Hi, Gideon."

Gideon's eyes flew open at the sound of Eddy's voice. He stood on the dock, his smile strained, as if unsure his presence would be greeted with cruelty or kindness.

"Hi, Eddy," Gideon replied as he sat up straighter. He motioned to the chair next to him. "Why don't you take a load off?"

Eddy bounded toward the chair as if propelled from a slingshot, his smile warming Gideon to the bones. "I didn't want to bother you, but I wanted to come by and tell you I'm going to college."

"Eddy, that's great. How are you swinging it financially?"

"Colleen helped me. She's been great. She got me a full scholarship to Stoneybrook Community College. She's promised when I'm finished with the two years there, she'll help me get into a four-year school."

Gideon wanted to ask about her. How was she? Did she look beautiful? Did she ask about him? Again regrets radiated through him. "What are you going to study?" he finally asked instead.

"Just general stuff at first." Eddy's gaze was oddly defiant. "Then I'm going to focus on criminology. I'm still going to be a private investigator. If I'm half as good as you, I'll be a success."

For a moment Gideon couldn't speak around the lump in his throat. He realized Colleen had been right. He'd spent the last three years of his life running, afraid to love again, afraid of what any love might cost him. But Eddy wasn't Anne. Colleen wasn't Anne. And if he turned his back on the love they offered, the price he'd pay would be dear—a lifetime of regrets.

"Well, I don't want to be a pain. I just wanted to let you know what I was doing," Eddy said as he stood up. With a wave, he started down the ramp to the dock.

"Hey, Eddy," Gideon called after him.

Eddy turned. "Yeah?"

"Don't be a stranger."

Eddy's face lit up like a Christmas tree, and again a lump formed in Gideon's throat. "Sure, I'll be in touch," he said, then turned and continued on, a happy lilt to his jaunty walk.

Gideon managed to sit still for a full minute before he realized he couldn't stand it any longer. He had to see Colleen. He had to see if he had blown his chance for happiness with her. He had to know if it was too late for them, too late for him to rebuild his life using love instead of regrets.

Within a short time he was parked across the street from her duplex, fear keeping him captive in his car. What if she didn't love him anymore? What if she had changed her mind? He wouldn't blame her. She'd bared her soul to him, spoken of her love, and he'd turned his back and walked away.

He shook his head, dislodging these thoughts, knowing there was no way Colleen's love could be so fickle. He saw her so clearly now and knew no matter what her upbringing, no matter the similarities of background, Colleen was a much different person from Anne. Colleen was a woman committed to helping people, a woman who loved with her heart and her soul. A woman who loved him.

The fear inside him fell away. He stared at her house, shrouded by the darkness of night, a single light spilling from the living room window. It was like a beacon of hope, the light of love, and it beckoned to him.

He reached for his door handle, but froze as he saw a dark figure race furtively from behind a tree toward the side of her house.

Pounding with adrenaline, Gideon eased his car door open, stepped silently out, then eased the door closed again.

He stood perfectly still, eyes trained on the side of the house as he wondered if he'd really seen something or only imagined it. Around him the night was quiet, but not silent. Autumn leaves skittered along the street, and a dog barked someplace in the distance. He narrowed his eyes, watching...waiting. Again he saw a flash of movement, and with the stealth of a cat, Gideon ran after it.

As he rounded the corner of the house, he saw a tall figure at one of the bedroom windows, the screen half torn away. Gideon didn't take time to introduce himself or wait for explanations. With a low growl, he tackled the intruder around the waist, both of them tumbling to the ground.

The man was about Gideon's size, and fought back, attempting to free himself. Gideon grunted as a knee found his stomach, but he didn't release his hold.

They grappled for what seemed like an eternity, an even match of strength that had them both gasping and grunting with exertion.

"What's going on?" Colleen's voice, high with near hysteria, penetrated the sounds of grunts.

"Call the police," Gideon gasped as the intruder sagged in apparent defeat. "This creep was trying to break into your window."

"I'm not a creep," the intruder said. "I'm her brother."

Colleen gasped, and Gideon released his hold and stood up. The man turned on his back, and Gideon found himself staring at Sam Baker.

"Sam . . . oh, Sam." Colleen ran to her brother and helped him to his feet. Once he was up, she launched herself into his arms, crying in obvious relief. "Thank God you're all right. You're alive. What are you doing here? Where have you been? Are you okay?" Questions tumbled out of her as she hugged him.

"Maybe we should take this reunion inside," Gideon suggested.

"Good idea," Sam replied. "The last thing I want is to be seen by anyone else."

Together the three of them went into the house. Colleen and Sam sat on the sofa, and Gideon took a position near the front door, unsure what to do. Sam's gaze on him was wary, and he didn't seem to relax until Colleen assured him he could talk freely in front of Gideon.

"Sam, where have you been? We've all been worried sick," Colleen said as she reached out a hand and grabbed Sam's.

"Everywhere," Sam replied, and Gideon heard the deep, abiding weariness in his voice. Sam looked at Colleen. "I didn't kill him, Colleen. I didn't kill Dad."

"I know that," Colleen replied, her gaze lingering lovingly on her brother.

"You know the police are looking for you," Gideon said.

Sam nodded. "The police and whoever was responsible for the murder. It's all a big mess. From what I've managed to piece together, somebody in the company was laundering large sums of money. Huge sums." Sam wiped his face with a hand and leaned his head back as if exhausted. "Whoever was responsible for the money laundering killed Dad, and I'm not giving myself up to the police until I know who did it."

"So what are you doing here?" Gideon asked.

Sam looked at Colleen again. "I need your necklace, the one Dad gave you. It's got a code on the back." He looked at Gideon. "I think my father knew what was going on, and he's got a file in the computer that will tell us who he suspected. I think that file will point a finger at his murderer."

"We found the file in your father's computer but couldn't access it," Gideon explained.

Sam nodded. "The file is also on the main computer at Baker Enterprises, but Dad apparently had it created by a genius. It can't be opened without the code."

"Why didn't your father just take this information to the police? Let them handle it?" Gideon still wasn't sure what to make of the situation.

"He was going to. He intended to talk to the police. He was murdered before he got a chance." He turned to Colleen. "Please tell me you still have your necklace."

She nodded. "We put it in a safety-deposit box. Did you take Bonnie's and Carolyn's? They were stolen...was it you?"

"No." A black despair swept over his features. "I wish it had been me. Unfortunately, I'm not the only one who has figured out that the key is in the necklaces. When I get yours I'll have two, and somebody else will have two."

"Why not give yourself up? Let the police sort all this out?" Gideon said.

Sam shook his head. "Whoever is responsible for all this mess has some of the police in his back pocket. I don't know who to trust. It's easier to trust nobody."

"What are you going to do?" Colleen asked softly.

"I'm not sure. I only know that as long as I have two of the charms, I have some bargaining power. Can you meet me someplace tomorrow with your necklace?"

Colleen nodded. "Then what?" she asked.

Sam smiled and placed a hand on Colleen's cheek. "Then I disappear again until I figure out some sort of plan." Gideon saw the love Sam had for his sister as Sam gazed at her. "Colleen, I've intentionally kept away from all of you. I've had to, and I'm sorry that I couldn't let you know where I was. I know it's been hard on you...hard on Julianne and Emily." A brief spasm of pain crossed his face, and Gideon knew he was thinking of his wife, his child. "The people who killed Dad are ruthless, and I'm afraid for all of you.

That's why we can't stay in contact. It would kill me if anything happened to all of you."

Gideon believed him. He believed all of it. What he saw before him was not a cold-blooded killer who'd taken his own father's life and was running from justice. What he saw was a man whose life had been ripped apart, a man who was afraid but determined to keep his loved ones safe and find the person or persons responsible for killing his father.

Within minutes they had agreed to meet at Gideon's houseboat the next day. Sam would arrive sometime in the morning, and Colleen would bring the necklace at some point in the evening. With luck, nobody would see Sam's arrival, and if Colleen was being followed nobody would think it strange she'd come to Gideon's.

Once the arrangements were made, Sam headed for the back door to leave. Gideon watched as Colleen and Sam hugged tightly, the bond of love between them apparent. Then Gideon and Sam shook hands and Sam disappeared into the darkness of the night.

Gideon saw the grief that darkened Colleen's eyes as she slowly closed the back door. She leaned heavily against it, eyeing him with a curious smile. "Thank you," she finally said softly.

"For what?"

"For not calling the police. For not turning Sam in."

"It didn't even cross my mind," Gideon replied truthfully.

"It did mine. I owe you an apology."

He looked at her in surprise. "Why?"

She moved away from the door, walked to the living room. Gideon followed, as always confused by her thought process. "Why do you owe me an apology?" he asked again as she sat on the sofa.

She folded her hands in her lap, gazing at them instead of at him. "While Sam was here I realized that if you took him in to the police, you'd be a hero." Her gaze met his. "You'd be the one who caught the man the police department couldn't get. There would probably be lots of publicity, money from new cases and guest appearances all over the country. You'd be a real-life hero." Again her gaze went to her hands. "For just a moment, I was afraid that the pull of all that glory, all that cold, hard cash might make you turn Sam in."

For just a brief moment, anger rose inside him at her words. What kind of a man did she think he was? The anger died as quickly as it had been born. Hadn't he gone out of his way to make her think he was just that kind of man? "You don't owe me an apology," he replied.

She looked at him once again, and this time tears sparkled in her eyes. "Just tell me it wasn't the money, Gideon," she begged softly. "Please, just tell me when you kissed me, when you held me, it wasn't because you wanted only my money. I just need to know that much...that it was me, not the money."

In that instant, Gideon realized how scarred she'd been by her brief marriage, and he cursed Jesse Jensen for the wounds he'd created. "Colleen, when I kissed you, it was because I wanted you, not your money. It *never* had anything to do with money."

Drawing in a deep breath, she nodded. "Thank you," she said with a quiet dignity that made Gideon's knees weaken with his love for her. She frowned thoughtfully. "So how did you see Sam breaking in? What are you doing here?"

"I was parked across the street, trying to get up the nerve to come in and talk to you."

"About what?"

"I've still got your dad's computer. I was wondering what you wanted done with it." The moment the words left his mouth, Gideon frowned, realizing he was running...again. "That's not true," he immediately blurted.

"You don't still have Dad's computer?" She looked at him in confusion.

"No. I mean, yes. Yes, I still have the computer and no, that's not why I really came by." He raked a hand through his hair, realizing it was time to jump back into life with both feet, knowing he wanted to jump back into love with the woman who stared at him, obviously perplexed.

"Gideon?"

"I...I've been doing a lot of thinking in the past week," he said as he paced the floor in front of her. "You were right about a lot of the things you said to me. I rolled over and played dead when I left the police force, and I've been playing dead most of the time ever since. I loved being a cop, and I was good at it." He stopped his pacing and remained in front of her. "I've decided I'm going to fight to get my job back."

"Oh, Gideon, that's wonderful."

"Wait...that's only the beginning." He saw the pulse that beat at the base of her throat, knew it reflected the sudden erratic beat of her heart, of his heart. "Colleen, I'm not a hero. I'm just a man who loves you."

Colleen felt as if all the air in the room had mysteriously disappeared. She gasped in shock, his words as unexpected as Sam's sudden appearance had been. She'd spent the past week trying to forget Gideon, wishing she'd never met him, realizing she could never forget him because he was in her blood, in her heart. She stared at him. Maybe she hadn't heard him right. "Pardon me?"

"Colleen, I love you. I want to marry you and make babies with you. I want to share my life with you." He stopped abruptly. Walking toward her, he held out his hand. "Come with me," he said.

Still reeling, afraid to believe his words, she took his hand and allowed him to pull her from the sofa. "Where are you taking me?" she asked as he opened the front door.

"Shh," he answered, a smile curving his lips.

He took her out into the middle of her front yard, then stopped and turned to face her. His disobedient, thick hair shone silvery with the light of the moon. His features were illuminated by moonlight. "You know I've heard it from good authority that it's absolutely impossible to lie if you're standing in the moonlight," he said, his voice a soft caress that filled her with warmth despite the chill of the night.

"I've heard that, too," she answered softly.

He wrapped his arms around her, pulling her close to him, so close she could feel the beating of his heart. He gazed into her eyes intently. "Do you love me, Colleen?" He stood still, as if holding his breath.

"Yes," she answered fervently, tears of joy blurring her vision. She wiped at them impatiently, wanting to drink in his moonlit features.

"Now, ask me."

She saw his hunger, his need for her shining from the depths of his eyes. She recognized it for what it was. Desire, yes, passion, yes, but so much more than that. She saw his love and had no need for the words. Wrapping her arms around his neck, she pulled his head down so her lips could taste his.

Love was in his kiss. Love so sweet, so pure, so strong it radiated through her. His mouth drank of her as he pulled her so tight against him their heartbeats melded, appearing to be one single strong heart.

Oh, how she loved this complicated, headstrong man. He might not know it, but he was her hero, a man she knew she would be able to depend on for a lifetime of happiness and love. And she would spend every day for the rest of their lives loving him.

As he ended the kiss, he gazed at her face. "You didn't ask me," he chided.

Although she didn't need it, she knew for some reason he needed to say the words aloud. "Gideon . . . do you love me?"

He raised his face to the lunar light, then looked at her. "More than life and forever," he said, and his lips once again descended on hers.

As Colleen returned his kiss, she tasted his promise, his commitment, his everlasting love on his lips. She felt as if she'd reached the end of a quest. What had begun as a mission to find Sam had ended in her finding a home in Gideon's heart.

Epilogue

They were married on the dock, surrounded by a small group of friends and fishermen. Margie was Colleen's maid of honor, and Eddy served as Gideon's best man.

"I thought Eddy was going to burst the buttons on his tux, he was so puffed up with pride when he handed you the ring," Colleen said, snuggling closer against her husband's side.

Husband. She thrilled at the word and raised her head to look at him. His hair, as always, was mussed, and his features were softened by the smile that curved his lips.

They had just made love, exquisite, soul-bonding love. He seemed so at peace, no shadows at all in his beautiful eyes. He gently brushed a curl of her hair from her forehead. "I'm sorry your family couldn't be here."

She shrugged. "Carolyn and Beau didn't count on the twins coming down with chicken pox, and who would have guessed Bonnie would be pregnant and suffering morning sickness twenty-four hours a day?" She smiled, hoping someday she would have the opportunity to experience the joys and ills of pregnancy.

"What?" He traced her smile with a fingertip. "What brings that smile to my wife's face?" He whistled softly. "My wife. Just the words give me such a thrill."

"I was just thinking how nice it would be to have a little boy with your eyes."

"Hmm, and a little girl with your laugh." His fingers trailed down the side of her face, a caressing touch of infinite love. At the same time a cool, salt-tinged breeze swept in through the window. Laughing, Gideon grabbed the blankets and covered them, pulling her closer against his body. "I can't believe you wanted to spend your wedding night here on the houseboat."

Colleen smiled, pleased with their new living arrangements. During the week they would stay in the duplex, and on the weekends they would stay on the houseboat. "On the nights I stayed here, I thought about being here in your arms. The whole room smelled of you, and I longed for you to get off that sofa and come in here with me. I dreamed of you making love to me while the boat rocked softly beneath us."

"Oh, Colleen, I hope I can always make your dreams come true," he said softly. "I just wish I could make things right with Sam."

"Gideon, we gave him the necklace, and he has our trust in his innocence. It's out of our hands. It's up to Sam now, and there's nothing more either of us can do for him." Colleen's heart ached at the thought of her brother, but she knew she was right. Sam's future was not hers to manage, nor was it Gideon's. Somehow, someway she had to believe that Sam would be all right. Besides, although it made her feel horribly selfish, she was so wonderfully filled with her own future, with the man holding her close.

"I have a wedding present for you," Gideon said.

She looked at him in dismay. "Oh, no, I don't have one for you."

He grinned, a lazy, sexy smile that stole her breath away. "Darling, just moments ago you gave me one heck of a wedding present."

A blush warmed her face as she realized what he was talking about. She elbowed him in the ribs and giggled.

He yelped in mock pain, then rolled over and grabbed a bag from under the bed. Immediately she smelled the familiar yeasty cinnamon scent. "Cinnamon knots? How did you ever get Elda to bake them for you?"

"I told her we'd raise her rent if she didn't."

"You didn't," Colleen gasped with a giggle.

He laughed. "No, I didn't. Actually, I think Elda was honored to make them for us." He opened the bag and reached inside. Withdrawing one of the sweets, he offered it to her.

She took a bite, then he took one, and a thrill of shared intimacy rushed through her. "Have I told you lately that I love you?"

"Yes, but that's one thing I'll never grow tired of hearing."

"Gideon, I love you," she whispered.

He smiled. "I think it's appropriate that we're having cinnamon knots on our wedding night. It's symbolic of our lives intricately tied together with love." He gave her another bite, then popped the last of it into his mouth. "And now, I have a favor to ask you."

"What?" Her breath caught in her chest as his eyes darkened, deepened with desire.

"Would you mind giving me my wedding present again?" A wicked smile lit his face as his hands caressed her nakedness beneath the covers.

"Why, Mr. Graves, I'd be delighted," she replied breathlessly.

As his lips claimed hers, she tasted the sugary sweetness of cinnamon and the fevered heat of his passion. More than anything, she tasted love.

* * * * *

What do women really want to know?

Trust the world's largest publisher of
women's fiction to tell you.

HARLEQUIN ULTIMATE GUIDES™

I CAN FIX THAT

A Guide For Women
Who Want To Do It Themselves

This is the only guide a self-reliant
woman will ever need to deal
with those pesky items that
break, wear out or just don't work
anymore. Chock-full of friendly
advice and straightforward,
step-by-step solutions to the
trials of everyday life in our
gadget-oriented world! So, don't
just sit there wondering how to
fix the VCR—run to your
nearest bookstore for your copy now!

Available this May, at your favorite retail outlet.

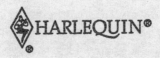

HARLEQUIN®

FIX

MILLION DOLLAR SWEEPSTAKES
AND EXTRA BONUS PRIZE DRAWING

SWP-ME96

SOMETIMES BIG SURPRISES
COME IN SMALL PACKAGES!

Bundles of Joy

AN UNEXPECTED DELIVERY
by Laurie Paige

Any-minute-mom-to-be Stacey Gardenas was snowbound at her boss's cabin—without a hospital or future husband in sight! That meant handsome, hard-nosed Gareth Clelland had to deliver the baby himself. With the newborn cradled in his arms, Garth was acting like a proud new daddy—and that had Stacey hoping for an unexpected proposal!

Coming in May from

BOJ596

FORTUNE'S Children™

In July, get to know the Fortune family....

Next month, don't miss the start of Fortune's Children, a fabulous new twelve-book series from Silhouette Books.

Meet the Fortunes—a family whose legacy is greater than riches. Because where there's a will...there's a wedding!

When Kate Fortune's plane crashes in the jungle, her family believes that she's dead. And when her will is read, they discover that Kate's plans for their lives are more interesting than they'd ever suspected.

Look for the first book, *Hired Husband*, by *New York Times* bestselling author **Rebecca Brandewyne**. PLUS, a stunning, perforated bookmark is affixed to *Hired Husband* (and selected other titles in the series), providing a convenient checklist for all twelve titles!

FREE
Keepsake
Bookmark

Launching in July wherever books are sold.

SILHOUETTE... Where Passion Lives

Don't miss these Silhouette favorites by some of our most distinguished authors! And now you can receive a discount by ordering two or more titles!

SD#05849	MYSTERY LADY by Jackie Merritt	$2.99 ☐
SD#05867	THE BABY DOCTOR	$2.99 U.S. ☐
	by Peggy Moreland	$3.50 CAN. ☐
IM#07610	SURROGATE DAD	$3.50 U.S. ☐
	by Marion Smith Collins	$3.99 CAN. ☐
IM#07616	EYEWITNESS	$3.50 U.S. ☐
	by Kathleen Creighton	$3.99 CAN. ☐
SE#09934	THE ADVENTURER	$3.50 U.S. ☐
	by Diana Whitney	$3.99 CAN. ☐
SE#09916	AN INTERRUPTED MARRIAGE	$3.50 U.S. ☐
	by Laurey Bright	$3.99 CAN. ☐
SR#19050	MISS SCROOGE	$2.75 U.S. ☐
	by Toni Collins	$3.25 CAN. ☐
SR#08994	CALEB'S SON	$2.75 ☐
	by Laurie Paige	
YT#52001	WANTED: PERFECT PARTNER	$3.50 U.S. ☐
	by Debbie Macomber	$3.99 CAN. ☐
YT#52002	LISTEN UP, LOVER	$3.50 U.S. ☐
	by Lori Herter	$3.99 CAN. ☐

(limited quantities available on certain titles)

TOTAL AMOUNT	$_____
DEDUCT: **10% DISCOUNT FOR 2+ BOOKS**	$_____
POSTAGE & HANDLING	$_____
($1.00 for one book, 50¢ for each additional)	
APPLICABLE TAXES**	$_____
TOTAL PAYABLE	$_____
(check or money order—please do not send cash)	

To order, send the completed form with your name, address, zip or postal code, along with a check or money order for the total above, payable to Silhouette Books, to: **In the U.S.:** 3010 Walden Avenue, P.O. Box 9077, Buffalo, NY 14269-9077; **In Canada:** P.O. Box 636, Fort Erie, Ontario, L2A 5X3.

Name:_____

Address: _____City:_____

State/Prov.:_____ Zip/Postal Code:_____

**New York residents remit applicable sales taxes.

Canadian residents remit applicable GST and provincial taxes.　SBACK-MM2

V Silhouette®
TM

You're About to Become a *Privileged Woman*

Reap the rewards of fabulous free gifts and benefits with proofs-of-purchase from Silhouette and Harlequin books

Pages & Privileges™

It's our way of thanking you for buying our books at your favorite retail stores.

PROOF OF PURCHASE
SR-PP130
Offer expires October 31, 1996

Pages & Privileges ™

**Harlequin and Silhouette—
the most privileged readers in the world!**

For more information about Harlequin and Silhouette's **PAGES & PRIVILEGES** program call the Pages & Privileges Benefits Desk: 1-503-794-2499